Secrets and Lies
in
El Salvador

~ Shelly's Journey ~

Contents

Prologue

After spending my life chasing a dream, running from one state to another, then from one country to another, I finally see what life is about. Today, my first son was born. I had not expected or planned for this; I had no idea that this would be such a beautiful experience. This woman, who nursed my wounds and loved me, better than any rich woman ever could, has given me a son. Of course, I have a daughter back in the States, but it is not the same. Her mother died giving birth, and quite honestly, I knew I could never forgive the child for this. It is not right, I know, but it is the truth.

Maria Elena named our son Roque, though she didn't give him my last name. Perhaps she was trying to protect him. I have so many people after me, more than she knows, more than I even know. I love a good fight, especially when it is against a rich SOB who thinks *he* has all the rights and I have none.

Maria Elena has been so sweet and good to me, but I must move on. It's what I do, what I've always done. If I stay still, stand in one place too long, someone *will* kill me. I hope she will understand. I will always love her and I will do my best to take care of my son, but I must move on to my next adventure.

Cuba, 1962
Roque Dalton
Though I hardly know him (okay, honestly I don't

know him at all), my father has always given me what he thought I needed. He made sure my mother could afford to send me to the best private schools, which in El Salvador means Catholic. And there was always food on the table. My mother and I didn't feel much like eating, though, because we didn't have what mattered most in the world – I didn't have my father and she didn't have her husband. Though by all rights, the rich were correct – I *am* a bastard child. Winnall Dalton never married my mother. And me, I didn't really have a father though I did benefit from his money, however ill-gotten it was. And finally, I chose to take his name.

Why my mother didn't give it to me the day I was born, I'll never know. She wouldn't talk about him no matter how much I begged. But his name might have saved me much undeserved suffering. *Dalton* is definitely not a Salvadoran name, so students and teachers alike may have treated me better if I had only had that name.

But that treatment was fodder for the fire of passion that has become my poetry, so I suppose I can say, "Everything happened just as it was meant to." How else would I have learned to understand the plight of my *compañeros*, the *campesinos*?

I will continue to learn to fight, to know how to take up arms against those who oppress my people. I will return to El Salvador, my "Tom Thumb" country. I will fight to the death if I must, for my beautiful little country. *¡Patria libre ó morir! ¡Vencéremos!*

Prague, Czechoslovakia, 1965
Miguel Marmol

"Yes, Roque," I tell my friend, my *compañero*, my comrade, "my life has been difficult, *pero no es nada* compared to my people who had to stay, who had no way out."

Roque is writing down my story, which he considers a very important one, but I must make sure he includes the story of my people, of our people. Despite being half gringo, Roque is as Salvadoran as I. He loves our people as I do, maybe more. The world must know the tragedy and heroism that is and always has been my people's history. Of course, Roque and I look forward to the day our own brothers and sisters will read this story, but we know that it may be some time before that happens.

"We were hungry. We were always hungry. But *we* had access to avenues others didn't. The only reason I had to work as a child is because of my mother's pride. When my maternal grandmother saw my ugly mug, she couldn't stand the fact that my mother had slept with a married, dark, ugly Indio! Okay, married, that was one thing; she could have dealt with that. But the fact that she brought into the world a child who was darker than her daughter? That was unforgivable! My grandmother had prided herself on the fact that she had cleaned up our family's bloodline by marrying a Spaniard. She spent her entire life bragging about this wonderful Spaniard who had changed her destiny.

"So for many years we got by the way most Salvadorans got by, any which way we could."

I can tell Roque is getting anxious. He wants all this background; he wants to get down my entire life. Of course, he wants to know what life was like before the massacre, but he also wants every detail about how we formed the party and how we got the word out about the strike, and what happened. He wants to be sure we have time for me to tell him about the organizing of the national peasants' strike and the ensuing massacre of 1932. He wants to hear the entire story of how I helped organize the peasants, how I got to know Farabundo Marti, and how the strike turned into a bloodbath because the army threw all of us – the organizers, that is –into jail the day before the strike was scheduled. He wants to know how so many of our Indian and Mestizo brothers ended up dead.

So, I continue with my meager life because it represents the life of so many Salvadorans at that time, and even today.

"Sigue, compañero. Está bién. Dime todo lo que vos te acordás." So I do continue.

"There were many people walking from town to town, offering to do whatever: repair our shoes; work on our humble shacks; pick the coffee, if we'd had any land to grow it on. I dreamed as a child about helping them all. I dreamed of lining the roads with trees so they wouldn't have that sun beating down on them all day. Hah! What a child I was! Even then, I was already a Communist!"

But suddenly I feel a profound sadness, thinking about my mother, not just because she's no longer with us, but I'm thinking of that bastard she let live with us.

"Miguel, please tell me, even if it's difficult, *especially* if it's difficult. This is what the world needs to know."

"Yes, Roque, I know. Just let me calm myself down for a minute." I take some deep breaths and wipe the tears from my eyes. "I told my mother I was going to kill Julian if he continued to beat her. It was a lie, of course, but she believed me. So she decided to leave him so that I wouldn't spend the rest of my life in jail. We now had no money and I no longer had a job, since

I was fishing with that *hijo de puta*. On top of that, there was an earthquake around that time so things got more horrendous for all Salvadorans.

"My grandmother finally took us in, though. I guess her love for her daughter outweighed her disgust of my ugly mug and dark skin. Plus, I had two sisters who must have had a different father because they were pretty. Besides, my *abu* was getting old and would need someone to care for her soon."

Roque is shifting anxiously again, so I try to think of something that might wake him up. "I finally was back in school. I was very intelligent, you know. The older folks, the ones who had been to school, loved to argue with me ... about politics, World War II, especially. I was finally studying history again. And was the smartest in my class. Of course, the others – students and teachers alike – still hated me. I was the darkest one in the school and they had the same prejudice against themselves as my grandmother had.

"*Abu* tried to keep me out of the sun, but I was defiant. Every chance I got, not only was I in the sun, but I would take my shirt off. So my entire upper body would get tanned. I remember her beating me when she caught me, on more than one occasion.

"We saw little of my mother during that time. She was growing fruits and vegetables: *güisquiles*, *yuca*, and mangos. And making friends with the weavers and the tailors. A group of them went into San Salvador every week to sell their goods. I think mother was glad to have an excuse to get away from *Abu*, but she missed *us* terribly, and always brought back candy or a little toy for us.

"Roque, do you want to get a coffee or better yet, some Czech *svařák*? I won't be here much longer. I want to enjoy the little bit of time I have left here. Besides, we need a little break. We can continue at the café," I suggest.

"*Si, si, compañero*, just don't forget where we left off."

Prague is a beautiful city, full of history and culture. But there's no place as beautiful as El Salvador, despite all the hardships and bloodshed. I miss the sun and the brightly colored clothes, though I imagine you seldom see my people in their native clothing anymore. After 1932, the Indians kept all their native accoutrements hidden away in the bottom of their trunks.

Chalatenango, El Salvador, 1975
Roque Dalton
Marcial has rejected me as a soldier. He says I have more important work to do, as a poet. But I refuse to accept this. I will find a way to fight. Yes, I am a poet, but I am just as much a Revolutionary. A poet needs his inspiration, his muse, and mine is the armed struggle. Without the struggle, I am nothing. Without my people, I am nobody. I will always remember that "the eternal spring continues in you (and me), *compañero*."

A Few Months Later
The day of my death has come. I accept death. I embrace it just as I have embraced life – with great gusto, with the fervor of a man who knows he'll go to heaven. In truth, though, I don't know where I'll be heading. Will I be able to continue writing this poetry in heaven? Will they want to read it? I think hell is a much better place for a poor poet like me. The devil

will toast me and laugh, and cry out, "Hah, you thought you made a difference! You thought they would love you and know the truth! You are such a stupid little poet! They couldn't understand how profound you were, how prophetic you were! If you had been around when Christ was here, they would have nailed you up there next to him, you fool!"

I accept hell. Shit, I'll make my Revolution *there*! I'll make that frickin' devil be sorry he wanted me in his burning embers. Besides, I can take the heat, just as I always have here in my beloved El Salvador. I can take the mocking, satirical remarks from the devil and all his accomplices.

Ay, though what saddens me is the stupidity of my brothers here in El Salvador. How could my own comrades-in-arms believe the shit the CIA and the death squads and the secret police have said? I always told them this would happen. What do they think? Would a spy tell them how he would spy? Would a traitor give up what would allow him to commit treason?

Ay, what will become of my people with idiots like these at the helm? If they do manage to organize the peasants and the workers and get them to fight and win *their* Revolution, won't they betray them anyway for the price of some fame and fortune?

Oh God, I can only hope you are there. I can only hope you will take care of my people, finally. Here, God. Not there, not after death. Because after death means after torture, the worst of tortures, the torture of seeing all that you love crushed at your feet, often by those you trusted most.

Please, Lord, take care of my people. Give them some peace. Give them some joy! Let them make love in the woods next to a waterfall. And bring the product of that love into a world of great beauty.

Let them kill me, Lord, but let my people be free from their misery.

Bang! Bang! Bang! "That son of a bitch will never betray us again. Now we can get on with our Revolution the way we know it needs to be fought. No more stupid little poet telling us how we need the ignorant peasants organized and fighting too."

"That stupid *cabrón* Padre Landarech helped us keep track of him with all his praise."

Roque – lying dead now, though his Revolutionary spirit lives on

I knew the army's secret service would take all my poems. Padre Landarech never got to see a single one. So when all is said and done, I betrayed myself, all in the name of gaining absolution for my sins. "And the wages of sin is death," he would have told me. He would have said, "Embrace it, my son, as you would a beautiful woman, because death and salvation are better than any beauty to be found here on earth."

Yes, Father, I embrace death, I do. I only wish I could take back all those times I hurt my beautiful and faithful Aida. If only I could be completely sure my sons know how much their father loves them. If only I could send messages from beyond the grave. What a difference I could make then!

Chapter 1

Becoming Chele

San Salvador, El Salvador, 1981

As Shelly steps out of the plane into the Salvadoran sun, the heat slaps her in the face and almost takes her breath away. She drops her passport with the claim form inside and watches it thump, thump, thump, as it hits each step all the way down the metal stairs. She had only wanted to block the sun from her eyes. *This is not a good sign*, Shelly thinks.

She wipes the sweat off her forehead as she looks down the steps to see one soldier checking off names while the other soldier looks at the passengers' passports. She notices that the soldier with the clipboard is holding a small handgun underneath it.

She walks down the metal stairs, picks up her passport, and has to run to catch her claim form before it flies off into the distant mountains. She hadn't wanted to make any quick moves that might make the soldier pull out his gun and use it. But she has no choice. As she approaches the men, she feels a shudder go down her spine and finally wonders if she is doing the right thing.

"*¿Nombre?*"

"Shelly Marie Smith." At least she has the sense not to mention the name Dalton, her mother's maiden name, although it is the custom here to use both parents' last names. Not only is it dangerous to be associated with the name Dalton, because of the Leftist poet who, though dead, was still considered "enemy

1

number one" by the government, but Shelly has also sworn never to mention that name again. Victor had carried on about the possibility of Shelly being related to the Left's hero, until Shelly finally called her mother and asked her. That was the last time they had spoken. Shelly's mother was brought to tears and still Shelly did not know if the American father of Roque Dalton could be her grandfather, though her gut feeling is that he was. Which would make Roque her uncle, and his sons her cousins.

When the soldier asks Shelly her occupation, she blurts out "Journalist" without considering the problems this could cause.

"*¿Periodista?*"

"*Si,*" Shelly answers, already realizing she should have taken Lori's advice and said anything *but* journalist. Lori had told her to just say she was a waitress, but even though that was the only work Shelly had ever done, she could not bring herself to say that word: *waitress.* That's part of the reason she is here, to forget about her past. If she had not been a waitress, she might have avoided getting raped. She would not have been in the street so late at night.

"*¿Y porqué estás aquí?*" the taller soldier asks. Shelly notices he is using the familiar you. *This soldier is being disrespectful. What did I do to deserve this already?* Although Shelly's grasp of Spanish is excellent, she wonders if she said something she shouldn't have.

"To visit family," she answers, trying to remain calm. Speaking English seems to help, so she hopes these soldiers understand her.

"¿Por cuánto tiempo?"

"I'm not sure. A month, maybe two," she lies.

"¿Y qué tiene usted alli?" the soldier asks, switching back to formal Spanish. But he looks at her suspiciously. "Are you planning to photograph the war?"

"Oh, no ... *no, solo retratos.* Portraits of *mi familia* and their friends. No, sir, I won't be taking this out to any war. I won't even be going near it. God, no." Shelly can feel the sweat trickling down her back. She hopes the soldiers don't notice the beads of sweat on her forehead.

"¿Cuánto dinero trae con ústed?"

Shelly laughs, "About a hundred bucks, sir." When the soldier just stares at her, she says, *"Perdón, señor— cien dólares."* Fortunately, the peace groups agreed to deposit the money directly into Mr. Gonzalez's bank account so she wouldn't have to carry it and take the chance of it being stolen. That gave them more time to collect donations too.

"You can go now," she is told, but as she walks away, she hears one soldier say to the other, "We better alert the authorities to keep an eye on that one. Something just doesn't sound right."

Shelly walks as quickly as she can without looking obvious. As she steps into the air-conditioned airport, the cool air feels like a winter breeze. She wonders why the passengers had to walk outside from the plane. *Are they that far behind the times here?*

She finds what she is looking for. The restroom. And realizes that it would be okay, her walking so quickly; they would just think she had to pee. She runs by the lady taking care of the restroom and goes into a stall. But the woman walks up to the stall door, knocks, and asks *"¿Usted necesita algo, señorita?"*

"No, gracias, señora. Estoy bien."

"Anything you need, señorita, I am here. *Cualquier información, solo me pides."*

"Information!" Shelly shouts, then quiets herself down. What kind of information could this woman think she wants? Or needs? Barely in the country five minutes, and she is already shaking with nervousness. *Fear* would probably be the better word.

She pulls out the little package Lori had slipped her at the New Orleans airport. The note around the watch, an awfully large watch, reads: "Someone will take you to see Carlos. Then you'll know what to do." A heart, and signed, "Lori."

Shelly lets out a yell. "What the hell? How can she do this to me?" She realizes it is a miniature camera, a spy camera.

"¿Todo bien, señorita?" the lady says.

"Yes, ma'am. Everything is fine," Shelly says, knowing full well the woman doesn't understand a word of English. Shelly realizes that her main defense here will be to pretend she doesn't understand whenever a problem comes up. "Sorry, ma'am, I don't speak Spanish."

"Vaya pués," she responds. And Shelly remembers the first time she heard that expression. Victor, the Salvadoran, who had tried to convince her not to go, had said those words whenever he was resigned to Shelly's determined reasoning. Victor, the Guanaco, who had taught her so much about his country,

although—she suddenly realizes—not enough. She should have tried to learn more.

Shelly leaves the restroom, ignoring the female informant, or whatever she is. She hands her ticket to a well-dressed young man, who brings her the bag she had carefully packed a full three days before she left New Orleans. Lori had laughed at her, saying, "It's not that big a deal, Shelly. You can do it the night before, or the morning of." But Shelly had been given so many warnings about what *not* to wear and what *not* to take that she felt like she needed a year to decide. In the end, she decided that taking her Nikon was a danger she would have to live with, but the jeans and shorts would have to stay in New Orleans.

"*¿Señorita Chel-le?*" says the man trying to steal Shelly's bag.

"*¿Señor Gonzalez?* Yes, I am Shelly."

"I knew that pretty, blonde, green-eyed girl had to be you as soon as I saw you." Shelly's long hair is pulled up into a bun, and she knows that without her jeans, she looks like a proper young woman. *No more hippie girl for me. Not while I'm here.* For a split second, Shelly frowns, mourning her former self. She wonders if she'll ever be that old self again.

"It is so nice to finally meet you. I hope you haven't been waiting long," Shelly says in the most polite Spanish she can muster. The entire time she spent in New Orleans, she tried to find people to practice her Spanish with. But after about two sentences, they'd always switch back to English. Shelly actually got more practice in Rochester. As a waitress, she met many young Latinos who knew almost no English. Most of them washed dishes night and day, so there was little time to learn the language of the country they had escaped to. El Salvador was going to be the real test.

"Don't worry, Miss *Chel-le*, we haven't been to the airport in a long time, so we came early to look around in the shops and be in the air conditioning," responds Mr. Gonzalez. "*Dáme tus bolsas*, but first let me give you a hug."

Shelly already knows she likes this man and is going to be comfortable staying in his family's home.

He grabs her bags, but she protests. "I can carry my own luggage, Señor Gonzalez. Thanks, anyway." They are having a tug-of-war with her suitcase and carry-on.

"Don't worry, Miss *Chele*, I am a gentleman. I will not be seen walking with a woman who is carrying her own bags. People will think I'm a brute. Did you think they would place you with a rude family?"

"Oh, no, sir. It's just that we don't have many gentlemen where I come from," Shelly says with a laugh.

"You don't have to worry anymore, Miss ..."

Shelly interrupts him. "Sir, the 'Miss' makes me feel old. Could you please just call me Shelly?"

"Yes, if you will call me Juan ... well, Juan Sr. since my son is a junior. Now, you must meet my beautiful family."

"Okay, Juan it is." She is wishing she had worn one of her sundresses from New Orleans, but Lori had made her promise not to bring them. She said that in countries like El Salvador (third world countries is what she was implying), people were much more careful about what they wore. "God knows," she had told Shelly, "one wouldn't want to be confused with a poor Indian!" Shelly had laughed with Victor about this statement, but Victor swore there was a tribe of blonde-haired, blue-eyed Indians living in the countryside with no knowledge of any other language except the indigenous language of the Pipil Indians.

So Shelly gives in and allows Señor Gonzalez to carry her bags, like any proper Salvadoran man would. She follows him and her bags over to the only clunker in the parking lot, and the entire family jumps out to meet *la americana*. Their 1971 dark blue Oldsmobile looks as if it has been through the war. Actually, she supposes it *could* have seen a few battles from what Lori had told her about her host family and the neighborhood they live in.

"Señorita *Chele*, oops, I forgot. *Chele*, this is Señora Gonzalez ... Isabel, the love of my life."

"*Mucho gusto, Señorita Chele*," she says as she gives Shelly a big hug. It is obvious to everyone Shelly isn't used to the Salvadoran warmth and hospitality. Shelly knows of the stories about the North Americans being cold, so she tries her best to look like she is completely comfortable with all the physical affection, but this is not going be easy, not after being brought up by a mother like hers.

"Don't you know that a healthy person needs at least eleven hugs a day?" Mr. Gonzalez asks Shelly. She smiles.

"*Mucho gusto, Señora Gonzalez, y muchas gracias* for sharing your home with me." Shelly is sure she is going to like Mrs. Gonzalez too. It occurs to her she may even grow to love this family.

"*De nada, niña*. And you can call me Isabel."

Another person calling me niña! A Nicaraguan woman she met in New Orleans had explained to her that she should not take offense. She said it was a way of showing affection. She also told her it was a compliment on her beauty, her perfect youthful skin, so Shelly decides to let it go.

"And this *niña* is the other *amor de mi vida, Leticia Consuelo Gonzalez.*"

"You can call me Letty. *Mucho gusto* and welcome to El Salvador, hermana." *These people are so sweet. Sister, girl.* Shelly already feels like part of the family, like a long-lost relative. Shelly is sure her mother would never welcome a stranger like this.

"*Y último pero no menos importante es Juan Jesus Gonzalez Hern—*"

"*Juan Gonzalez*, at your service. *Cualquier cosa que 'vos necesites, solo me lo decis, oís?*"

Wow, not only is he offering his help, but he also uses vos *instead of* usted. *These people really do want me to feel like part of the family.* Though she still feels awkward accepting his hug. She remembers her mother getting angry at her father because a woman from her church hugged him after he fixed her washing machine, and then when she offered, her father had refused to take any money from her.

They all pile into the Oldsmobile and head to the Gonzalez home.

"*Chele*, there's one more family member at home. We realized that if we all came, someone was going to have to ride in the trunk on the way home, so Abuela volunteered to stay home," Mr. Gonzalez tells her.

Shelly is quiet now, taking in everything around her. She is glad to have the excuse of Spanish being her second language, as she can tell this family is not used to people being quiet. Victor had warned her about that, after she had explained to him that he shouldn't be upset; it was normal for people, Americans at least, to keep doing whatever they were doing when their guests came in. Later, though, Shelly had wondered if it really *was* normal. Maybe her family was different from the rest.

Everything looks less orderly and less clean the further away they get from the airport. Shelly tries to appear peaceful as she looks around at all the disorder that is San Salvador—all of El Salvador, for that matter, as she understands it. She tenses up, though, whenever they have to slow down at the army checkpoints. The soldiers are boys, not men—she can see that—but the uniform alone is intimidating. Fortunately, since they're coming from the airport, they don't wonder why these dark-skinned people have a blonde with them. Shelly prays that they don't decide to stop the car and search it.

Everyone is talking at—not to—Shelly, which she would normally find extremely nerve-racking, but she takes it all in stride.

Chapter 2

No jeans

Shelly tries not to show her shock when they pull up to the house. Victor had warned her that middle class looks different here. On the corner of the block is a bombed-out building. It appears to Shelly like it might have been a little market.

"*No se preocupe de eso*. The army thought the guerrillas were hiding out there, so they blew it up. The family still sells basic necessities, but you have to go to the back door of their home now," Juan Sr. tells her.

Don't worry about it? No big deal? Shelly is taking deep breaths like she was taught to do by one of New Orleans's well-known healers.

"The army thinks the insurgents live and carry on activities in this neighborhood so we've been hit especially hard," Mr. Gonzalez says as he carries Shelly's bags to the door, "but they won't bother us now that we have *una norteamericana*, living among us."

Shelly hopes Señor Gonzalez is right about that.

Before Mr. Gonzalez can open the door to their home, Shelly turns her head to look down the other side of the block, where she sees a red car. And suddenly, BOOM!—it blows up. There are shards of glass flying everywhere. Shelly jumps and lets out a yelp. She stares at everyone's faces, but they do nothing. She falls flat on the ground, the way Victor taught her. The entire family looks at her without moving from the spot where they were standing.

Shelly stands and brushes herself off, hoping they do not see her flushed face. *I am beginning to think they chose the wrong person for this assignment.* Of course, Shelly had fought to be chosen for this. There were only two other people, both guys, who wanted to come. In the end, they most likely chose Shelly because she was a woman, not because she was the best photographer. She was the best though, at least when it came to making portraits. She had a way with people; she made them feel comfortable.

Out of the front door comes the woman Shelly assumes is Abuela. *"Y aqui está the other much-loved person en ésta casa,"* Mr. Gonzalez says.

"Juan, you shouldn't talk about your mother-in-law that way. People might think you actually like me," she says, winking at Shelly. Shelly smiles shyly at her.

She puts out a hand and begins to say, *"Señora ...?"*

"Yo soy Abuela, no matter who you are. Everyone who lives *en ésta* casa calls me Abuela. Even my son-in-law calls me Abuela." Then she gives Shelly a hug like she's never had before. *"Es un placer* to meet you, *Chelita."* Shelly feels her breathing slow down to its normal rate, no longer scared she might have a heart attack. *I guess I am not the only one who can make people feel comfortable.*

"Come in. I've been cooking for two days so you can try many of our Salvadoran delicacies. Did you know we have the best food in Latin America?" She laughs as she says it, but Shelly believes her. Victor had taken her around to all the Salvadorans he knew, so she had tried *pupusas*, of course, *masa* filled with delicious cheese and black beans, or *chicharrón*, which she did not eat. She told Victor that pork was the worst of all meats, that there was no way she would ever eat that. Victor had said that she was going to be served a lot of pork, that it was considered the best food and what Salvadorans always served their guests.

Mr. Gonzalez walks over to Shelly, after putting her bags inside a room and closing the door. *Possibly my bedroom?* Shelly wonders. He puts his arm around Shelly as he begins telling her who gets up when. Shelly glances back at his wife to see if she is getting jealous, but she is smiling. Shelly realizes that she is going learn a great deal from this loving family. Victor was not a hugger, so Shelly wonders if it was Victor who was atypical or this family. Whichever it is, she'll find out soon enough.

Inside, the Gonzalez home is exactly what Victor had warned her of: *humilde*. In English, *humble* has a slightly different meaning. In Spanish, it's a nice way to say *poor*. Actually, according to Lori, it meant someone who isn't educated and therefore doesn't have a good job or life. Because Señor Gonzalez is a union organizer, he lives a humble life. He lives a life similar to his union members. He chose to help others have a better life, which means giving up many luxuries for himself and his family. Most American kids would feel bitter if their father chose a life like this for them, but this family seems closer than any Shelly has ever met.

"Welcome to our humble home, *Chele*," Mr. Gonzalez says as he steers her into her bedroom. "I wish we could give you a room of your own, but you will have to share Letty's room." Shelly's bags are already in there. She discovers later that Abuela is sleeping in Juan's room during her stay.

"*Todo está bien, Señor. Gracias,*" she tells him, wishing she could go in and close the door, calm her nerves, and collect her thoughts.

Instead, Abuela brings her some *yuca con chicharrón*. "Some people say mine is the best in El Salvador, so that is what I am giving you first."

Shelly is feeling embarrassed, as she is the only one being served food. She has been a vegetarian for most of her life, but Lori told her that it wasn't going to be possible here. In New Orleans, she had tried to eat meat, but it literally made her sick.

"*Gracias*, Abue ... la." Shelly is tripping over her tongue. The woman she had thought was her own grandmother had died a few short months ago. She hadn't even discussed this with her mother before she left, knowing that her mother preferred living a lie. The woman Shelly had called *grandmother* all her life was really Shelly's great-aunt, sister to her grandfather who Shelly is almost certain escaped to this country because he had gotten in trouble with the law. Shelly's grandmother, or her aunt, or whatever she was supposed to call her, had left Shelly with this knowledge that she never felt she could share with the woman her "grandmother" brought up as her own, Shelly's mother.

"Abuela, let her rest. She must want to freshen up and relax," Mr. Gonzalez tells his mother-in-law. He understands women better than Shelly would have expected. She walks into the tiny bedroom and closes the door, wondering if she should tell them she is a vegetarian. This is exactly what Shelly needed, to be forced to pare down her life to the bare essentials.

Letty comes in and whispers, "I told them you needed a nap so you could have time to put your things away, *con tranquilidad* ... and take a nap too, if you'd like." She winks and shuts the door.

Shelly is thankful for their understanding. Her head is swimming. Suddenly she remembers the small package Lori slipped into her bag at the airport. She told Shelly to keep it close until she could find a place to hide it. She takes out the spy camera that looks like a large watch and thinks how unfair it was of Lori to put not only her but this entire family at risk, without so much as a warning. Shelly crawls on the bed and tucks it under the mattress on the side by the wall. She puts her camera bag next to the bed, hoping that she will be able to start shooting some pictures very soon.

Letty has left her two drawers to put her clothes in, which is perfect for Shelly. She puts the four crisp new cotton blouses and three skirts in one drawer. In the top drawer, she puts her new cotton panties, four of which are still in their bag. Two bras. And two pairs of shorts that she's brought. She knows ... well, she was told, not to go out in public in shorts, but she figures she could at least wear them around the house. She places her nightgown under her pillow, and smiles, remembering her grandmother—she's already decided this woman will always be her grandmother. *Besides, great-aunt is not that far away on a family tree.* She remembers seeing her every morning in her nightgown and robe as she fixed the family breakfast. Shelly has always worn her T-shirt and underpants to sleep in, much to her mother's disapproval. *Mother would be proud to see me finally wearing a nightgown.*

And not a single pair of jeans, her clothing of choice since the time her mother had allowed her to choose her own clothes. In New Orleans, she had given up her jeans because of physical necessity; the humidity was unbearable. She would have felt like she was in a sauna in her jeans. Here it was a matter of social etiquette, really. Lori had said that many assumptions were made about women because of how they dressed. She insisted that Shelly didn't want to draw that kind of attention to herself. Despite her bad judgment with the spy camera, Lori had probably given Shelly some good advice. It's better to be too careful than not careful enough. Today's mishap at the airport had taught her that. She wonders if she should tell Mr. Gonzalez, just in case.

That night, Shelly wakes to the sound of helicopters and *bombs*. Yes, she is quite sure she hears bombing. She walks into the living room where Abuela stands, apparently praying.

"Abuela, are they bombing something out there?"

"Hush, *mi niña*, no, of course not. *Son cojetes*."

That makes no sense. How could they be fireworks? Besides, there was no mention of any celebration. Shelly goes back to bed, realizing she will never know the truth.

15

Chapter 3

Conversations and questions

Abuela immediately seems to like Shelly. Shelly senses that Abuela has no idea what a North American girl is like, but Shelly is sure Abuela knows she is different, not like any stereotype she has ever heard about. She seems to know that it is Shelly's nature to be sweet, shy, and respectful. And totally unimposing. Shelly has always tried not to make waves, except when it came to her mother, of course. She can't help it. Wherever her mother is involved, one never knows what crazy idea Shelly might come up with next. All just to show her that she is her own person. She is sure that if her mother had her way, she would mold her into a miniature of herself. She is not about to allow that to happen.

Abuela wants to cook for Shelly, to make her feel comfortable, to make her feel at home. Shelly understands. After all, that is what her own grandmother had always done. So she tries not to make a big deal out of Abuela serving her and no one else. She finally decides she will do her best to try to eat the meat she is served, and to always remember to be grateful to Abuela and to this entire family.

Abuela's guard is down with Shelly, and as Shelly soon learns, so is everyone else's. Abuela begins telling Shelly all her secrets, secrets she has kept to herself for as long as she can remember. *Forever, really ... because Abuela has never been able to talk to anyone,* Shelly is realizing. She learns early on that Abuela has kept secrets from her mother, from her daughter, and even from her grandchildren. *But Abuela knows I won't stay forever, so she figures her secrets are safe with me.* Abuela seems to have no idea, though, that everyone else is thinking the same thing.

So Shelly becomes "the keeper of secrets." She doesn't mind though. In fact, Shelly seems to savor each little tidbit of information, each detail. Shelly will occasionally ask questions but most of the time she doesn't need to. She just listens attentively. At one time or another, she realizes, Abuela will overhear every member of the family telling Shelly their secrets. This is how Abuela discovers who her family *really* is.

Every time Shelly is alone with Abuela, she begins asking her many questions: *What is it like in the US? What is my mother like? Are women very different there?* Shelly answers with great patience and detail, as she can see Abuela is a curious woman who probably would have traveled the world had she been born into different circumstances.

She tells Shelly about the 1932 massacre that she witnessed as a child, a secret she has kept all her life, until now. Although Shelly is using the excuse of photographing Abuela, she soon realizes that Abuela needs no pretense or excuse to talk, not to Shelly anyway.

"It was 1932. I was in Sonsonante, where I grew up with my mother and father. It was a small town, but at that time there was some money there. Coffee was becoming a huge cash crop. Americans were beginning to drink it every day, so some of the big landowners were making large profits. The money trickled down to the rest of us. My family, in particular, was doing well, as Papa was in the transport and building business."

Shelly asks Abuela to change positions, to face the window, then to face away from it. All the while, Abuela keeps talking.

"Mother warned me not to take walks alone just before dark. I wish I had listened to her. Instead, I have to spend the rest of my life trying to forget what I witnessed. I was passing the *mercado* as everyone was finishing putting away their goods. It had been a good day, so there was little left for the *campesinos* to take home. Their children had come to help after school, as they always did, but the mothers and fathers carried most of what remained in baskets balanced on their heads."

Shelly makes another adjustment, closing the curtain so the light is softer. It makes Abuela look younger.

"Suddenly, I heard young men, boys really, shouting, '*¡Ay vienen los comunistas!*' I recognized a couple of the soldiers, as they were local boys. They were not in uniform, but I knew it was the army, not the Communists. What followed was enough to make those peasants and their children shake with fear whenever they heard the word *comunista* or *comunismo* again."

Shelly doesn't want to disturb Abuela, is afraid that she might stop talking, so she pretends she is still taking photos, even though she can think of no other poses in the place they are at now. She decides that another day she will find a better—or at least, a different—location. For now, she just listens.

"Don Fernando de Jesus was commanding the *comandante*. I would never have believed it if I had not seen it with my own eyes. He would tell the commander something, then the commander would shout to the soldiers, *'¡Matále a éste!'* Kill this one! Rape that one! Grab the baby! I could not believe that Don Fernando could be this cruel. These were his workers. Every one of them had worked his land at one point or another. He even sent them after Paula's parents, Don Pablito and Doña Consuelo. To this day, I am sure Paula does not know that her ... lover had her parents killed. She does not know the evil that lies in the heart of the father of her child. I pray that she never learns."

Shelly believed that calling a grown person their name with "*ito*" at the end was a way to minimize their status, but Victor had insisted that wasn't true, that it was a way of showing *cariño*, affection. They had argued about this at length.

"They killed them both, chopped off Señor Pablito's head and cut the baby out of Señora Consuelo's belly. I had to tie my scarf around my mouth and hold it with both hands so that my screaming would not be heard."

Shelly is stunned. She has no idea what to say. She wishes she had stopped her, but there's no turning back now.

"And all this happened because? I don't know for sure and I didn't dare ask, but I heard whispering that some man named Farabundo Marti was helping the peasants organize. They were going to take over some of Don Fernando's land. It was land that was lying fallow, so why should Don Fernando care if they used it? They could have grown enough food to feed all their families and Don Fernando still would have had his coffee. They never would have abandoned their *jefe*!"

After thinking for a second or two, Shelly decides to say, "Abuela, the guerrillas call themselves the Farabundo Marti National Liberation Front."

Abuela ignores her comment.

"I think this Farabundo Marti called himself a Communist, and it was obvious to everyone that this wasn't his doing. But even if logically the *campesinos* understood that it was the army behind this horrible scene, emotionally and psychologically, they would always relate this bloody massacre to the Communists. And the many children who would never speak of this, would never be spoken to of this, would never hear uttered the word *massacre*, did not even know enough to comprehend that the army would lie. They would always blame the Communists."

Shelly doesn't know what to do, so she just stares at Abuela. She believes Abuela must know that this is related to today's fighting, but why did she choose to tell of this to Shelly? *Shouldn't other people, other Salvadorans, be made aware of this? Shouldn't she be telling this story to someone else, someone who could see the connection and do something about it?*

Chapter 4

Café con leche

Shelly's first few days in El Salvador have been better than she could have hoped. Besides the car blowing up, there has been no other violence or bloodshed. Her time with Abuela is a comfortable way to acclimate herself, to practice her Spanish, and to learn some history from a personal perspective. The rest of the family goes out: to work or school. Shelly wonders how Abuela occupied herself during these times, before she got here.

It is Shelly's third day alone with Abuela. She has listened as Abuela talks about her life, sharing all her secrets with Shelly. Abuela sets Shelly's *café con leche* in front of her, along with some *pan dulce* she had gone out to buy while Shelly was taking her Salvadoran style shower (which is not really a shower at all, as you have to scoop the water out with a small pot and pour it over you).

Abuela sets down her own coffee ... without milk. She loves *café con leche*, but she explains to Shelly that women her age save the milk for the young. "They need the nutrition more as they are still growing, or if they are older and working, they need the extra energy. There isn't enough for everyone, even with the dried milk that I buy at the colonel's home." Shelly remembers this box because it said A Gift from the People of the United States on the front in big letters.

Shelly went with Abuela when she bought it. She got so upset that Abuela had to tell her to go home.

Shelly could not believe that an army colonel was making money off something the US government sent there to help the poor. When Abuela came back home, Shelly yelled, "It's bad enough that my government sends money and arms here to help the army fight its own people, but the little bit of help that really *should* give the poor some relief? Even that goes into the pockets of the people with the power!" Abuela didn't say a word. Shelly could tell that she agreed with her, but didn't know what *she* could do about it.

Abuela sits, but doesn't touch her coffee or sweet bread. She has a serious look on her face and it seems to Shelly, looking at her now, that she has been waiting for the right moment.

"*¿Eres Católica?*"

Shelly looks up at her. She cannot lie.

"No, Abuela. No, I am not Catholic."

"*¿Eres Cristiana?*"

Again, she has to tell the truth.

"No, Abuela, I am not Christian. I've never been baptized."

"*¿Pero, si, crees en Dios?*"

Do I believe in God? Honestly, Shelly doesn't know how to answer that question. She and her mother have gone round and round about this. It isn't so much that she doesn't believe, but she's sick of all the hypocrisy of the so-called Christians in her town, families pretending to be normal while hiding secrets of children born out of wedlock, infidelities, and outright abuse. And now, being here, considering what God is allowing to happen here, Shelly wonders how anyone in this godforsaken country could believe in God, but she also knows that Abuela is not the person to have this conversation with.

"*Si, Abuela, por supuesto.* Of course I believe in God." Shelly hears her breathe a sigh of relief and notices her shoulders relax a bit. Despite telling her a half-lie—*or is this what they call a white lie?*—Shelly feels better. Whether her time here would swing her to the left or right on this question, she doesn't know, but for now Shelly has made an important ally in Abuela, an ally who might prove valuable during her stay here.

Chapter 5

Talking about war

"His name is Don Fernando de Jesus Lopez Garcia." Abuela tells Shelly. "People here think he is over one hundred years old, but he is in his eighties. He is from my home town."

"And why do you want me to photograph him, Abuela?"

"Oh, you'll see, *vas a ver*," she tells Shelly.

As they walk into his beautiful ranch home, Shelly can see why Abuela thought she should photograph not only the old man, but everything in his home. It is like a museum.

"*Don Fernando, esta es mi amiguita*, the *americana* I told you about. She wants to photograph you, but I want you to tell her your story so she has a better sense of who you are. Okay, Don Fernando?"

"*Si, niña Maria*. Of course."

Shelly looks at Abuela. "Your name is Maria?"

"Maria Elizabeth. Everyone always called me Elizabeth. But he probably doesn't remember so he just calls me Maria."

As Shelly begins taking shots of Don Fernando from different positions, he begins to talk.

"It was 1932 and I had no choice but to tell the army where the peasant uprising was coming from. I had to inform them who was organizing these men and women to fight. If I had not done that, my family could lose everything that my father and grandfather worked so hard to earn."

Shelly stares, knowing that this is going to be a different kind of story, not sure that it is one she wants to hear.

"My grandfather got those thirteen hundred hectares when he married my grandmother and the two families merged their land. He worked more than fifty years from four in the morning until six in the evening to make sure the coffee beans were planted and tended to. When it came time to pick the beans, he himself made sure it was the exact ripeness for the perfect flavor. After the peasants picked them, the beans would be baked in the sun for the ultimate bouquet and flavor. The entire process, including getting the beans to the mill where they were ground, took a full year. As soon as the coffee was sold to the American company, the cycle began again."

Although Shelly is getting some beautiful images, prize-worthy shots, she doesn't feel right.

Something doesn't feel right.

"I should have learned more from my grandfather so I would not have to depend on these peasants. They cannot be trusted to be loyal, yet I have to trust them. *Pablito* tells me when it is the right time to plant. He shows me when the beans are ready to be picked, and only he knows how long they need to roast in the sun. I am going to have to find someone else to do this now."

Shelly looks at Abuela, wondering why he is talking like it is today this is happening. Abuela says, "Shush, *no se preocupe*. He doesn't know that fifty years have passed. In his mind, it all happened yesterday."

"It is unfortunate that *Pablito* and his wife Consuelo were with the other peasants planning the revolt. Jose, my secondhand man after *Pablito*, had even seen them with Farabundo Marti when he came to our village. What could they expect? Did they think I was just going to turn my land over to them?"

Don Fernando is going back and forth, talking between past and present.

What has Shelly most surprised is not that he seems to be lost in time or even the horrible words he is speaking, but this is the man that Abuela watched while he commanded the army to kill her neighbors.

How can she continue to talk to this man? How can she give him any comfort in his old age?

He continues. "I didn't mean for them to die, but what could I do? Tell the army, 'Spare those two. They're okay'? That not only makes no sense, it would have been downright stupid on my part. They could have turned around the next day or the next week and taken over my land. They had to die too. This is war we are talking about."

Don Fernando looks at Abuela and asks, "Niña Maria, how is my son? Paula is hoping to see him."

"Está bien, señor. I hope he will be coming to see his mother soon. And you too."

Shelly feels nauseous, but she doesn't want to talk to this old man or even use his bathroom. "Abuela, I need to go home now, please?" she begs.

"Si, mi amor. Vamos a la casa ya." And so they do go home. Shelly doesn't ask Abuela anything. In fact, she doesn't say a word and neither does Abuela. But it

suddenly occurs to Shelly that Don Fernando may be the father of Juan Sr. The idea sickens her so much that she doesn't bother to ask Abuela if it is true. She figures that, sooner or later, the truth will come out.

Chapter 6

Enlisting

Shelly is trying to read the newspaper and learn a little more Spanish when Letty runs into the house crying. Shelly sees her face and is immediately concerned. She wonders if someone has died. Maybe someone she knows has been killed in the war.

"Letty, what is it?" Shelly asks, giving Letty her complete attention.

"My brother says he's joined the army!" Letty screams as she unfolds into Shelly's arms. Abuela comes out of Juan's room. Letty immediately runs to her grandmother.

"This is the worst day of my entire life. He says he's doing it for me, but I don't want him to! How can you do something for someone else when they don't ask for it?" Her words emerge in a tumble, and Abuela has to help her remember to breathe. She is trying to soothe Letty, but it is obvious that she is just as upset. *She hides it well, but she knows what this means, even more than Letty does.*

"I don't care if I go to medical school. I want my brother back. I want him to always be Juan, this Juan, *el Juan que yo conozco*, not some monster who has witnessed cold-blooded murder."

She stops for a second, then begins crying even louder. "Or worse, a monster who has ordered poor, humble *campesinos* to murder someone: a mother, a

28

child, a mother with child! How can I go on and live my life if my brother does this? How can I become a doctor in good conscience?"

Shelly thinks, *he could die*, but she decides it's best to keep this thought to herself if they are ever going to calm Letty down. "Letty, are you sure he's not just considering it? Maybe he wants someone to offer him another option. Maybe he said it to see ... I don't know, to see if anyone has a better idea."

"Oh, *Chele*, I so wish you were right, but I saw him near the barracks ... and he's already joined. He was carrying his uniform. Abuela, he looked so proud ... he really thought that I would be happy about this, happy that he could help me."

Letty is bawling again and Abuela stares at her, wanting to comfort her, *but too upset herself to be able to comfort anyone*. And Shelly feels totally helpless. This was one eventuality that she hadn't imagined encountering.

"I will never take one centavo from him! I will be a beggar in the street before I would take his blood money!" Letty runs into her room, slamming the door, and Shelly can hear her sobbing into her pillow. She looks at Abuela, but she sees a blank face staring back at her.

Chapter 7

A burden

"I'm going to die for her if that's what it takes," Juan Jr. tells Shelly. "I never had a chance to go to school, to do something with my life. My father was so involved with his union organizing and not talking to his father. It never occurred to him to ask my grandfather for help ... help for me, his only grandson ... my father's only son."

Shelly is getting used to everyone telling her their secrets and their pain, but she is beginning to feel that keeping all these secrets is a burden she does not want to bear.

"I don't know what I'm going to do with my own life, so I try to help Letty since she does know. I don't know if I'll ever get married or how I would support a family. Of course, I don't want anything to do with this army, but what can I do? Who am I? Who will I become? What is my path? I have none! I am no one!"

Shelly has no idea what to say, so she continues taking photos and listening. Juan finally says, "I shouldn't blame my father for everything, though. I had a girl who loved me, who was going to have my baby. And I said no ... I told her I was too young to be a father and a husband. I thought I had better things to do with my life. I am such an idiot!"

It occurs to Shelly that there is much more to Juan than meets the eye.

"I saw Carmen yesterday and I almost cried. She looked so beautiful standing in the sunlight with a baby on her hip and holding the hand of her little girl. She rushed into the *panadería* and came out with a box of various kinds of sweet breads. I thought I was out of sight, but she caught a glimpse of me ... she stood absolutely still for about five seconds while her daughter chatted away at her."

Shelly has stopped photographing and is staring at Juan. She knows she should at least pretend that she is capturing his image, but she is too engulfed in his story to worry about it.

"How could I have let this woman, the woman of my dreams, go? Now, looking back, it makes no sense at all.

"She had missed her period so we went together to the clinic. She was so happy when she told me she was pregnant. Then she looked at me. There was no way I, a seventeen-year-old about to graduate from the *secundaria*, could be a father. I didn't have a job or money or any idea how to care for a wife and child. I didn't know then about my grandfather, that he was so wealthy, or I would have done things differently. I barely scraped up enough money to pay for the abortion.

"Carmen had cried and cried. 'Aren't you planning to marry me?' she asked me between gasps of breath. Of course I wanted to marry her. That was all I ever wanted from the first time I laid eyes on her. But I wanted to do things right. I wanted to get a good job, *then* marry her, *then* plan our family."

Shelly continues to stare, thinking about her own

abortion, and how Steven had offered to marry her, despite knowing that it was not his, that Shelly had been raped. Shelly couldn't imagine how this young woman must have felt, knowing that Juan did not want to take responsibility for what he had helped create, yet claimed to love her.

"She had the abortion, but she never spoke another word to me after that day. Six months later, she married the son of her father's business partner and within a year they had a baby girl.

"I should write a book called *How Not to Ruin Your Life*. Lesson Number One: When the woman you want to marry says she's pregnant, do *not* mention the word 'abortion.' Even now, just thinking about it, I feel sick to my stomach. I hate that word! In a perfect world, it would not exist!"

Shelly thinks to herself, *Amen to that*!

"Carmen told me I was condemning her to hell and still I insisted. So, if anyone is condemned to hell, it should be me. If God is good and just, Carmen will go to heaven and I will be punished not just now, in this life, but in the afterlife too.

"So you see, Shelly, I might as well die in the army. If Letty can benefit from my mistakes, can go on to become a doctor, at least my life will have been for something. At least someone will have benefited from my miserable existence."

Chapter 8

Blaming others

Shelly manages to find Carmen and convinces her that she should let Shelly photograph her. Curiosity has gotten the better of her and she wants to hear Carmen's side of the story. Maybe it is because she too has had an abortion or maybe it is something else. But Shelly had gotten enough information from Abuela to find Carmen's home. And, surprisingly, Carmen has agreed to meet with her and to be photographed.

Carmen's home is beautiful. Shelly thought no one lived like this in this third world country, demolished by war. Of course, there are the old homes, like the one Don Fernando lives in, but this house has been recently built and looks like something out of Hollywood. Like everyone else, Carmen immediately begins telling Shelly all about her life.

"From the time Juan first told me about himself, his family, and his painful past, I let him know that I loved and accepted him exactly as he was. I told him we could build the life we wanted together, with our own bare hands, with our own wonderful brains, and with our hearts that would always beat as one."

Shelly realizes that she must still be in love with Juan. *So what about this husband of hers? What about this life and this home? These children?*

"Why then did he not take me as his wife when I became pregnant with his child? He swore that he was sure it *was* his child, that he knew I had never been with anyone else. His goddamned pride got in the way of both of our chances for happiness. Who cares if he never knew his real father's family? This is a fact he is unaware of, anyway. His grandmother confided this to me when she thought we were going to get married and have the baby."

Shelly is getting confused now, wondering what she means. *Not his real father? How could Juan be Juan Jr. if his father is someone else? And if, as she says, he doesn't even know this, it could not be the source of all his sadness and anxiety.*

"Who cares if his maternal grandmother was a maid who ... ? Well, this is all irrelevant. She's not his real grandmother anyway. But none of this should have mattered ... Not what he knew. Not what he didn't know. He had me. Shouldn't I have been all he needed? And my being pregnant with his child, shouldn't that have been a chance for a new life, a new family? A family that would allow him to write history anew?"

Shelly continues taking photos of this bittersweet scene: a gorgeous woman living what seems to be an idyllic life. But the truth seems to be something totally different.

"No, Juan wanted to wallow in his misery. He wanted to continue to blame everyone else for his problems. That way, he could continue to do nothing, accomplish nothing, and it was not his fault. That way, he had an excuse to not take chances, to not try."

Shelly identifies with what Carmen is telling her about Juan, realizing that she, too, has been blaming others for her problems.

"He never suspected that the day I walked out of that clinic, I was still pregnant. The entire staff conspired with me to make it look as though I had an abortion. I would not be damned to hell because he did not have the guts to be a husband and father. Besides, even if they *had* agreed to do an illegal abortion, I was too far along. I was already five months pregnant."

This takes Shelly by surprise. *So she did not have the abortion. What happened to the baby?*

"If I could have lived with myself, it would have been much easier to lie about when my last menstrual period had been and have the abortion. I could tell my mother would have preferred it, but I just could not bring myself to do it. Of course, my father never knew. My mother said it would break his heart, but I knew better than that. My father would have considered me a disgrace to his family name, not worthy of his love.

"So, I went to the convent as my mother instructed me to do, until my baby was born. They promised me, my son, *our* son, would be given to a wonderful loving couple. They said he would be well cared for. I pray every night that they told me the truth, that my son is being brought up by a loving family.

"Against their wishes, I held him before he was taken away. I understand now why they insisted I not hold him. Maybe if I had never seen him, I could forget his face, his eyes. Maybe I would not remember every year how old he is, and maybe I would not look at every boy his age to see myself and Juan in his face. Maybe I could have forgotten him. He is the child from my one and only love. He was my happiness. With him and Juan, my life would have been complete."

Shelly thinks of *Romeo and Juliet,* and how she had argued with the Latino students in her class. She had told them that they were in love with the idea of *el Amor Imposible.* She had told them that they wanted to believe in something not real, rather than be happy with the life they had. It certainly seems to be true in this case. Carmen has everything, yet she is miserable.

"Instead, every day is a routine. I wake up and remind myself to be happy with this man I married, and with these two beautiful children. I remind myself that I have a great life. But I always remember that it is not the life I chose. It is not the life I imagined or hoped for. It is someone else's dream I am living. My husband could have continued until he met the woman who was meant to be his wife, not the one his parents chose for him. My parents chose him for me too. Instead, I would be in charge of my own life."

Shelly gets up quietly and sees herself out. She has no idea what to say, so she says nothing.

Chapter 9

Confusion

Juan Sr. or Señor Gonzalez, as Shelly calls him, had made a fuss about having Shelly photograph him. He had joked that no one would want to look at photos of an ugly guy like him. Shelly had laughed, and begged some more, not commenting on the fact that she thought he was very distinguished looking, that he was actually quite handsome.

Just like all the others, as soon as he sits down and Shelly pulls out her camera, he begins talking away.

"My son has joined the army and it is *all* my fault. Twenty years ago, my father gave me a choice ... though I saw it as an ultimatum. I chose the life of a union organizer. My father said he would send me to school and take care of my family, if only I would give up the idea of organizing workers."

Shelly is listening intently. This is the kind of story she wants to hear.

"I hated him for making me choose. It would have been very difficult, but I could have done both. Isabel could have finished her education and life would have been much better for our children.

"But I understand now ... my father's fears. They are the same fears I now have for *my* son. I want my son to live long after I am gone, to have children, and to be able to live with himself. My father was wrong in his assumptions, but I can see why he wanted a different life for me. He thought I could be killed, or worse, my family be hurt. And he thought I would have regrets, but I have had no regrets ... until now.

"If my father would have paid for my education, then I in turn could have paid for Juan's. He would not have felt he had to join the army. And we could have found a way to pay for Letty to go to medical school and still keep my family out of harm's way.

"But, I will not go to him again. I refuse to ask him for anything. I got my family into this mess and I will find a way out. My father will not hold all this over my head. He will not control who I am or who he is in relation to us. He has hurt my mother tremendously. I won't let him hurt me, or Isabel, or my children.

"Thank God Juan does not know that I am not his biological father. Otherwise, he would surely think that is the reason I have not gone to my father to ask for the money to get us out of these problems."

Shelly perks up. *This must be what Carmen was talking about.* She wonders who Juan Jr.'s father could be if it is not Señor Gonzalez.

"When I told Isabel I would marry her despite her being pregnant by another man, whose name she refused to speak, I made her promise to never ask about my family. To this day, no one knows that I am the bastard child of Don Fernando de Jesus Lopez Garcia. He is my father and his maid is my mother."

Shelly stands there in shock. So that horrible man she photographed *is* Senor Gonzalez's father. But then she wonders, *Why doesn't he have his last name*? The more Shelly learns, the more confused she becomes. She had been thinking that this was such a perfect family, so much better than her own. With her mother not wanting to know the truth about who she is and where she comes from, she had idealized this family because they loved each other enough not to allow the war to tear them apart. Shelly thinks about how her parents argued about religion and how Shelly should be brought up. Now, her own family's problems and secrets were starting to seem small and inconsequential compared to the Gonzalez family.

"I try to be good to my mother, but it is hard since she is the secret that I hold closest to my heart. Someday, I will go to her and ask her forgiveness, but it hurts to know that she has continued to live under my father's roof as his maid. Even after his legitimate wife died, she has stayed on, probably sleeping in his bed. But she has never become his wife."

Shelly thinks back to the old man's home and is unable to remember anything that left her with the impression a woman lived there. *Except the kitchen, but that would be true whether she were treated like the maid or his wife. Maybe his mother still feels like the maid?*

"My father said he would give her anything she needed, and me too, as long as she never told who my father was. As long as she remained his secret whore, I would have a good life. They made one huge mistake, though. They did not realize how much a three- or four-year-old boy could remember until he became old enough to understand."

Shelly wonders about this. If what Juan Sr. says is true, her own mother should have some memories buried deep inside her.

"I swore to my father I would never take a dime from him if he did not own up to his own actions. He had to take responsibility publicly by giving me his name, or risk having his secret told to anyone at any time. I have never told anyone, but I cannot take that SOB's money either. How could he hurt my mother the way he has, and how could *she* agree to such a thing?

"So, I hold these secrets knowing that I could help this young man, who has always been a son to me, and this daughter of mine who will soon be a woman. Am I doing the right thing? I no longer know what is right. I should be helping them in any way I can, but how can I go crawling to this man who never had the guts to be a proud father when I have been a proud father to a son who is not my blood? Oh Lord, please don't let anything happen to my son. Please help him see that there are other ways to manage in this world. Show him he does not have to kill to make a living."

Shelly stands quietly with her head down, praying along with this man, hoping that adding a second voice to his prayer might help.

Chapter 10

Strange comfort

Abuela told Shelly before she went to bed that she would be taking her to hear Monsignor Romero the next day. Shelly is happy that Abuela trusts her, despite knowing that Shelly is not a Catholic. Shelly's mother is Catholic, but Shelly decided she was more like her father, a believer in humanity, not needing something from another world to believe in. Shelly is happy that Abuela accepts her as she is, knowing that she is a good person; knowing that is what counts.

Abuela must know Shelly would not have come to this country in the middle of a war if she were not a decent human being; Shelly is sure of that. She even told Shelly that the American soldiers think they are here to do good; they just don't understand what's really happening.

Shelly can tell that Abuela has high hopes for her, that she believes Shelly will somehow let the world know what is happening in this country. She told Shelly that when she hears the archbishop speak, when she realizes how much he loves the Salvadoran people, then she will know that his words are important. Then she will remember all that he says and will carry his message to others.

Perhaps somehow she might even get the US government to pay attention to his message and realize that they are helping the wrong people. In this way, maybe Shelly can help end the bloodshed. Shelly had once thought this herself, but now that she is here, she realizes things are not so simple. In fact, sometimes Shelly thinks that she will be lucky to simply get out of here alive.

Shelly knows that Abuela has ridiculously high hopes for her, but she understands Abuela has always lived on hope and she doesn't want her to stop now, when there is little left *but* hope.

When they arrive at the cathedral, Abuela pushes them through the crowd. Making a stop at the holy water, Shelly tries to copy Abuela and the others, but they are so fast that she's not sure. She should know this; her mother is a Catholic. Shelly's parents had fought over this at length. Her mother wanted her to be baptized and christened and to go through confirmation. In the end, Shelly's father had won the battle, but Shelly now wonders if she and her father had lost much more than they had won.

Shelly dips her fingers in the water. *How many fingers? Does it matter?* She brings her thumb and two fingers up to her head, then her chest, then left, then right. She hopes she has it right.

Abuela gently guides her into a corner where they'll be able to see the monsignor. It is stuffy, hot, and humid. Shelly is surprised her claustrophobia hasn't kicked in. Instead she feels a comfort being in this particular crowd. That combined with the humidity makes her imagine what it was like in the womb. She feels warm and happy ... and protected.

"The cathedral feels safe despite recent killings and continued threats to priests," Abuela whispers to her. "Monsignor seems calm looking out from behind the curtain. The assassination of Father Rutilio Grande and other priests that he brought into the church, plus yesterday's killing, would have most of us hiding, but not our beloved Romero."

Shelly watches as the monsignor comes up to the pulpit now. Everyone is quiet; all she can hear is the swishing of clothes as the faithful shift their weight and cross themselves. Everyone who was seated stands. Shelly is disappointed, angry even, as she can no longer see this man that she had heard so much about. She has her camera in her bag, but she hasn't decided if she should take it out. Whether she takes any photos or not, she wants to see this man, the man who, all on his own, has gotten the word out to much of the world about what is happening here. He spoke at the Bishops' Conference and was a main speaker when they met to discuss a new kind of theology, one that said the poor didn't have to accept their lot in life. Shelly remembers the slides her professor had shown the class.

Romero moves his hands down like he is fanning a fire, and slowly everyone sits again. He looks humbled by his followers' respect and awe. Some younger men—"Priests from some of the faraway parishes," Abuela whispers to her, but Shelly misses what she said—move in quickly and adjust the microphone. Someone unseen must have turned up the volume.

It takes Shelly a minute to adjust to the Archbishop's formal Spanish. He speaks softly. "Today,

El Salvador is living through its own exodus ..." Abuela holds Shelly's hand close to her heart. Shelly can feel it palpitating. Shelly thinks, *She knows these are exactly the kind of words that anger the military. They want him to talk about the past, Jesus's time, not what is happening now.*

"... the injustices to which we are witnesses in El Salvador."

Shelly's hand is hurting. Abuela is holding it so tight against her chest, Shelly can't tell which heartbeats are hers and which are Abuela's.

When she finally begins to really focus on what Romero is saying, he is asking questions: "Why does slavery exist? Why is there marginalization? Why is illiteracy rampant?" Shelly had heard about Romero even back home, but all she knew was that he was part of a new group of the Catholic clergy that endorsed Liberation Theology. The Salvadoran and other repressive governments had immediately condemned their ideas, saying they were espousing Communism. They accused these priests of being Communists, masquerading under the cloak of the church.

"The true solution ... a better land distribution, a better administration ..." Romero doesn't fear for his life like the rest of us, Abuela had told Shelly the previous night, trying to prepare her for anything that might happen. Abuela said he told his followers that he is ready to die if God decides it is his time. But it is not God deciding who dies—it is the generals, the captains, even members of the government. Abuela had gotten agitated and finally said she was going to pray and go to sleep.

Hearing him now, though, Shelly feels the weight of his words, the power of his convictions. She can even understand the fears of the military and the wealthy. It is obvious that this man loves his people more than he loves life itself.

"No one is conquered, no one, even though they put you under the boot of oppression and repression ... Whoever believes in Christ knows that he is victor and that the definitive victory will be that of truth and justice!"

Shelly imagines he must have prayed and meditated on these words for days. *He must have asked God many times to speak through him.*

Abuela is getting so upset she is shaking. Shelly doesn't understand why. After all, she brought Shelly here. She knew what he would talk about. But then, Shelly realizes this is not about her. Abuela loves Romero. She loves him like the husband she never had. She loves him even more because her love is pure.

"In Tejutla ... they told me about a terrible violation of human rights." With those words, Shelly is beginning to comprehend. She too is scared for Romero. *That must be why Abuela is clenching her fists*, Shelly realizes. *She fears they will hurt him.* He is describing how "the military men in civilian dress and some in uniforms, opened doors, pulling people out in a violent way with kicks and blows from rifle butts."

Abuela is visibly shaking now. No one else has ever spoken publicly about these abuses. And until recently, the archbishop only spoke about the abuses when he was outside the country, where he was unlikely to be hurt.

Romero continues. "They raped four young women, beat their parents savagely, and threatened ... if they said anything ... they would have to bear the consequences." He begins to say the names of the victims who have been killed. "Jose Omar Sanchez, *¡Presente!*"

"*¡Presente!*" his followers sing out after every name.

The victims, he tells them, "will always be with us, in our hearts, but now they are with God; now they are at peace."

Romero goes on to describe the severe violence in response to a recent national strike. "... the military rulers. Let us hope that they will not be blinded by what they are doing with land reform."

Abuela is still shaking. Shelly notices beads of sweat on her forehead. This is what started this war, Abuela had told Shelly earlier. The peasants wanted land to grow their own crops in 1932, so they would not have to watch their children go hungry.

"I would like to appeal in a special way to the men of the army ... the National Guard, the police, and garrisons. Brothers, you belong to our own people. You kill your own brothers and sisters ... No soldier is obliged to obey an order counter to the law of God ... In the name of God and in the name of this long-suffering people whose laments rise to heaven ... I beseech you, I beg you, I command you in the name of God: cease the repression!"

As Romero drinks some water and tries to catch his breath, Shelly sees out of the corner of her eye, walking right through the open cathedral doors, someone with a rifle. She hears one loud BANG.

Romero is hit right between the eyes. He is down! Everyone is screaming. Abuela has fainted.

Shelly runs out the church doors in time to see the hooded man and his rifle entering the open door of an SUV. It has darkened windows and no license plate. Shelly thinks, *The assassin will never be caught. There will never be justice for this horrible murder.*

Chapter 11

Living and dead

Shelly watches as Abuela prepares for the funeral. Abuela says nothing. Shelly has no idea what to say to her, so she remains silent. They both drink black coffee and eat cheap white bread. Shelly guesses it is some kind of Catholic ritual, a type of penitence, maybe, but she doesn't ask. When Abuela stands at the door with her sweater on, Shelly knows it is time to go.

Shelly has never been in a crowd this large. As she looks in front of her, the people furthest away are the size of ants. And if she turns in any direction, it is the same. Her claustrophobia seems to have subsided, as she is breathing normally now. She is being carried along by the crowd. A few people are holding up photos of Romero; most have somber looks on their faces; others look scared. Shelly doesn't see any tears, which forces her to hold back her own. *What right do I have to cry*, Shelly thinks, *if these people, who loved this man so dearly, are keeping their tears in?*

Abuela has gotten word, somehow, that the monsignor's coffin is in front of the cathedral. There is a huge banner of Romero hung from the top of the cathedral. Shelly wonders how many people stayed up all night to get that made. There are young men and boys passing out small handbills telling about recent activities of the FMLN. Their faces are covered with big bandanas, much bigger than any Shelly has seen before, in green, black, and red.

Abuela is holding Shelly's arm. Shelly wonders if Abuela is worried that she might get lost, or if Shelly serves as simply her anchor on this, the saddest day of her life. Abuela had told Shelly that she considered Romero to be the man in her life. Since she never had a husband, she had devoted herself to the monsignor. And, of course, to God.

Suddenly, there is a loud boom! So loud and close that Shelly loses her hearing. Shelly looks around from left to right and back again. She sees that people are trying to run, to get away, but there's nowhere to go! There are people everywhere. Shelly notes how many of the people in the crowd are women. The men are trying to stop the women from falling and getting trampled. They all end up on the ground. People are falling on top of them. Shelly can see, but not hear; only a few are screaming. Whether the others are too scared to scream, she doesn't know, but she does notice a woman with something between her teeth, a hat maybe, as if she is trying to prevent herself from screaming. People on the ground are reaching up an arm, hoping someone will pull them up before they get trampled to death.

Shelly's hearing comes back slowly. She can hear faint noises like the lowest volume on a TV, and she hears a ringing sound. As she looks around for Abuela, she can hear again. She hears shouting and the scrambling of feet ... but Abuela is nowhere in sight. Then she hears a loud boom, then another. She realizes that it is gunfire. A few young men with guns are lying on the ground, keeping cover for the Green Cross as well as everyday civilians. Other young men are carrying the dead and wounded into the cathedral. Shelly knows it will not do any good to look for Abuela in this chaos, so she walks up the steps and into the cathedral.

Once inside the sanctuary, Shelly turns around to look out. There are thousands of shoes strewn everywhere. There are hats and papers, and the fliers and handbills she saw being passed out earlier. And people. Mostly women of every age, but the majority look to be grandmothers. The only people left are either dead or wounded. Rescue workers carry women on their backs; civilians are helping too. Shelly can tell who the civilians are because they don't know how to carry a body. It takes two of them, despite their being larger than the men wearing the Green Cross helmets.

Inside the cathedral, people are laying the dead— all women, mostly old—across the tiled floors. They line them up like in the photos Shelly had seen in her class. The professor said that it wasn't part of the curriculum, but he wanted his students to know what was happening, to not spend their life in ignorance. He'd wanted them to not to have an excuse to do nothing.

One of the priests is taking photos and Shelly feels a pang of guilt. She should be taking photos so he can attend to the living people, his congregation, and those of other priests.

Abuela had insisted Shelly leave the camera at home, claiming, "We will be too cramped for you to get photos anyway." Shelly wonders now if she'd expected this. It seems to Shelly that Abuela always knows what is going to happen next, even though, Shelly imagines, she always hopes she will be wrong.

As Shelly looks around, she sees an American taking pictures, too. His brown hair and white skin stand out against the bronzed, black-haired people here. There is a woman with him, writing stuff in a pad. She is asking others, *"¿Usted sabe quien es?"* Most of the time, they reply, "No, I don't know her." Some people are telling her who these dead women might be. She writes down everything they say, even when one piece of information contradicts another. As Shelly looks at these women and hears the people saying, *"Puede ser la abuela de—"* ("could be the grandmother of—") she feels nauseous. Suddenly, the room is spinning and everything goes black.

Chapter 12

Everything happens for a reason

Shelly sees Abuela looking through the window. An American is carrying Shelly. The young woman with him is Salvadoran. Abuela crosses herself. *She is giving thanks to God, Jesus, and her newest saint, San Romero.*

Shelly is embarrassed at being carried, so she closes her eyes when Abuela opens the door and shows them to her bedroom. When Abuela sees Shelly's chest heave, she crosses herself again. *She is thanking God for keeping me safe. Abuela could not handle calling my parents to come get my body. She could not have borne telling them it was her fault I was dead.* Shelly vows to be more careful in the future.

The American tells Abuela, "*Soy* John. She passed out in the cathedral. They told us she was staying at this house."

"*Si, si, si, ella vive aquí* ... with us. She was with me at the funeral. She was with me ... but I lost her hand. I tried to keep hold of her hand, but people were falling down all around us. Thank you so much for bringing her home," Abuela tells them.

Shelly realizes that despite all their differences, she is part of this family. She is sure that this old woman cares about her as much as her own grandchildren.

The woman tells Abuela, "*Soy* Cecilia, or Ceci. I am in charge of interviewing witnesses and families of the victims. We were trying to find out who the victims were. John was taking photos for me to post. She walked in and looked around. When she passed out, we started asking who she was. No one knew. Fortunately, we went in the right direction and found Miguel. If not for him, we never would have found your home. Of course, she would have told us when she woke up, but luckily we didn't have to wait for that."

"Oh, yes, Miguelito knows our family very well. Will she be alright?" Abuela asks. Shelly feels bad that Abuela is still worried. She should have had John put her down before they got here, when she first came to, but she was too embarrassed to say anything.

"Someone caught her when she was falling, so she didn't even hit her head. The Green Cross worker looked at her and said it was shock. She couldn't bear what she was seeing." John is speaking.

"*Grraaacciiiaaasss.* Can you leave your name and address with Abuela? I need to talk to you both." Shelly has sat up and is smiling. Since she seems to be alright, Abuela gets the information for her and says goodbye to this nice young couple. Shelly smiles, suddenly remembering the phrase, "Everything happens for a reason."

Chapter 13

Real work

After some soup and a good night's sleep, Shelly wakes up early to go see the couple who brought her home. She wants to thank them, of course, but mainly she wants to find out who they are and what they are doing. Maybe there's some way she can help. Abuela finds Miguelito and tells him to take Shelly to the Refugee Center.

When she arrives at the former storefront, she sees the buildings on each side have been bombed out. Miguelito tells her, "*Aquí está.* This old *mercado* is the Refugee Center now."

There are kids running in and out of the partial shell next door. They shout, "*¡Hola, Miguelito!* Come play with us."

He brushes his hand in the air as if to say, *I've got more important things to do. No time to play for me.* The children play with whatever they find. They are playing war. Even the girls pretend to be chasing and shooting each other. They make noises to imitate the sound of gunshots; they even imitate the sound of a machine gun. Shelly rushes inside the building marked Mercado Popular before she sees or hears anything else.

"*¡Chele!*" Cecilia calls, like she's an old friend. She rushes over to Shelly and hugs her. There are tired-looking peasant women sitting on old, beat-up metal chairs against one wall. There is a camera set up, but Shelly doesn't see the American or anyone else who looks like they might be taking photos.

"Cecilia—"

"Call me Ceci, please. When I hear Cecilia, I am always looking around for my mother, wondering what I've done wrong this time."

"Your English is perfect, Ceci."

"Oh, thank you. I love you already," Ceci says with a wink and a smile.

Ceci tells the women sitting around the room that she is taking a break. They look up but do not respond, or even acknowledge that she said anything. They look worn down, beaten by life.

Shelly realizes that she is probably not what Ceci had imagined in an American coming all the way down here, ready to suffer hardship. Shelly knows that people see her as naive, idealistic, and sheltered.

To some extent it is true, but there are many things that most people don't know about her, like the fact that she grew up on a farm, until her paternal grandfather died and the land and home had to be sold to pay off the loan. They discovered after he died that the farm hadn't made a profit in more than ten years.

Ceci tells her about John. "He was a conscientious objector. Rather than fight in the Vietnam War, he chose to spend his time in jail. As he learned more about the things your country is doing, he decided being a journalist was the best way to combat the lack of knowledge that most Americans have.

"None of that matters, though. I need someone to do the work John does not have time to do. And,

Chele, you are the perfect person for the job." She smiles and Shelly looks at her with the seriousness of someone applying for a job that they are in no way qualified for.

"But how did you know that I'm a photographer?"

Ceci looks over at Miguelito. "Miguel told us. He said you are always making portraits of the family."

"Yes, it's true, but I don't even know this boy."

"Oh, well, you will soon enough." Ceci smiles and winks at Miguelito.

Shelly says, "I won't be as good as John, but I promise to try my best."

"Well, Chele, you never know until you try, but I suspect you will be better at this particular job than John. He's used to being out where the action is. When he's here, I can tell he's just waiting for that next call and the chance to get out and do some real work.

"I began this project after the first massacre. When *campesinos* started arriving from the countryside, I managed to find two other people with the same idea. We found this *mercado* between two bombed-out buildings. The owner didn't care what we had planned; he just wanted to make some money. He knew he'd been lucky we were interested," Ceci tells Shelly as they both look around at these serious, unsmiling women.

Shelly knows this will not be easy, and she wonders how Ceci has managed to do this these past few years. She wonders if she's ever wanted to run away from it all, forget about her country and this war. She doesn't say anything, though; she simply listens as Ceci continues talking.

"John showed up about a year later, after two photographers had disappeared. He had to come either very early in the morning or very late in the afternoon, when there was not enough light to do his photojournalism. And of course, if there was work in other parts of the country, this would have to wait. That meant that some people did not get their photos taken. Someone could be out there looking for them and might not ever find them. As you can see, almost everyone here is female. Mostly mothers looking for their husbands or their sons ... and occasionally their daughters, although they usually know what happens to the young women and teenage girls."

Shelly looks at her, both wanting and not wanting her to elaborate. Ceci continues, seeming oblivious to the fact that Shelly has no idea what happened to the women and girls.

"The day before Romero was killed, John told me he could no longer do this work. He had been assigned to do more work in the countryside and would only be in San Salvador a few days a month. He was able to stay a few extra days to photograph the funeral, and then we found you. I say it was divine intervention, but John says it's just the one good thing that has to happen after a hundred bad things. He says it's a matter of odds."

Shelly thinks, *Yeah, John and I think alike. Nothing divine about any of this.*

"But when you ran into the church, we knew you were the newest foreigner to come to try to help our people. We saw how you looked at everyone—the priest taking the photos, the women who had been killed, John, and then me. You passed out after looking again at the women lying dead. We were very lucky to find where you were staying. Had we gone in any other direction, we would have had to find a place to lay you down until you woke up. Miguel? Is he related to your host family?" Shelly stares; she knows the family depends on Miguelito, but she has no idea who he is, whether he is a relative or not.

Shelly is looking around the storefront setup and she knows now it was the sight of the women that made her pass out at the cathedral. She feels a profound sense of sadness, as she looks around at the women lined up in chairs. She hardly notices the bare walls.

"Later, we found other kids playing in the street. They took us right to the Gonzalezes' door. I could tell you've spent time with these kids as they were all very worried about you."

Shelly feels her face warming from all this talk, which Ceci must notice, as she changes the subject.

"John is already gone. He's been sent to photograph some American and Salvadoran diplomats who are following up on the Agrarian Reform. He said he would be stopping at different towns on his way back, so I won't see him for about ten days."

Shelly tells her, "Don't worry. I can do all the work here. John should focus on getting photos that show the fighting. Hopefully, he can get some printed in the American and international press."

As Shelly looks around at these women, her heart sinks. Their faces are blank, as if they have forgotten the meaning of love. And hope.

"They are here to find their loved ones," Ceci tells her. "The ones who have survived and the ones who haven't. John and the other photographers take photos of all the bodies they find. They get close-ups of their faces and write down where they were found."

Shelly follows her out back, to the courtyard.

"We keep these albums here in the courtyard," Ceci says. "The women look for as long as they can stand to. Sometimes we'll hear one of them cry out, and we know she has just seen the face of her husband or son ..."

Shelly is relieved that she is speaking English so the women don't have more sadness piled onto their already terminally sad lives. *American women would have probably committed suicide if they had to endure what these women have endured,* Shelly thinks.

Ceci tells her, "We need someone to take photos of the women while I am writing down their testimony. All the photojournalists are too busy now. There's so much to do."

Shelly tells Ceci, "It's okay, I will do it. This is what I came here for. *Por éso estoy aquí." How on earth could I have thought I would be happy to find my place? How could anyone be happy about this*? Shelly is beginning to realize that she is not nearly as courageous as she had hoped to be. "Don't worry. I know how to do everything. I will take the photos, develop the film, and make prints ... But where is the darkroom?" Shelly asks, suddenly aware that it could not be in this building.

"You will take the film to the same place that John and the others go. It is about four blocks to the east. This is why we chose this building," Ceci says.

"But won't the journalists be there most of the time?" Shelly asks, realizing that there may be even more pressing work than this.

"All the foreign journalists send their canisters back for the workers at their home offices to develop. It's safer ... and faster that way." Ceci stresses the word *safer* and Shelly decides to wait until some other time to ask about journalists who have been killed. She sees that Ceci is worn down too, despite the fact she has found her sweetheart because of this war. Shelly imagines that she would rather the war never happened, even if it meant not meeting John.

Chapter 14

A wonderful moment

Shelly has been waiting for the right time to ask Isabel if she can photograph her. She knows all the family members better than she knows Señora Gonzalez, who leaves the house for hours at a time, never telling anyone where she is going and when she'll be back. Isabel is one of the most beautiful women Shelly has ever seen; she is only a few years younger than Shelly's mother, but she looks like she came from another generation—too old for Shelly's hippie ways, but too young to look and act like a mother whose life has already been determined.

As soon as Isabel sees the camera, she begins to tell her story. "We were in Sonsonante, where I was born and raised. It was 1952. My mother had managed to get me into the very prestigious *liceo*. My grades qualified me for free tuition and my grandparents paid for my books. I was the top student in my grade. Of course, they always recognized the male students, but I didn't care. I loved to learn. It was all I cared about … until the day I met Samuel."

Shelly knows that these images of Isabel will be stunning. She has already decided that she will no longer be Señora Gonzalez; Isabel is such a beautiful name and it fits her perfectly. Shelly is more excited than she has been in years. Capturing Isabel's image on film is what photography was invented for. *That and making a statement that makes a difference in the world.* But this was pure. This was perfection.

"From the first time I looked into Samuel's eyes, I

felt as if I'd known him forever. There was a familiarity that could not be explained. Later, he told me he felt the same sense of already knowing me, too."

Shelly also feels an excitement now, for the story. She can tell this one is special. "We studied together, tutored each other in our preferred subjects, quizzed each other, and fell in love with each other. We would meet at the library or go to the park. We'd go eat *pupusas*; we'd even go swing on the children's swings.

"One day, Samuel insisted on taking me to his favorite spot. He blindfolded me, he said, because he wanted to surprise me, but I believe what he wanted was my trust. He held onto my hips and veered me this way and that so as to avoid rocks and trees.

"Finally we arrived and when he took off my blindfold, the view took my breath away. From the hillside where we stood, we could see the volcano and the lake below it. Birds flew above us: parrots, *quetzales*, and crows. Samuel laid his jacket on the damp moss and sat down; he pulled me down beside him. We sat silently—looking—feeling—breathing in the atmosphere for a long time.

"Then I turned my face to him and he turned his to me. I don't know if I kissed him or he kissed me, but it was the most wonderful moment of my life. We made love there, the first time for both of us, and I fell deeply in love with him. I am sure he felt the same. Making love with him was like going home after thinking that you had no home. It was like being in Eden ... with no fear, no shame, nothing but goodness and beauty." *Wow, Shelly thinks, I guess Juan Sr. knows nothing of this. It would break his heart to know she loved someone more than she loves him.*

"For more than a month, we went to that paradise every day. Then one day, Samuel said he was taking me home to meet his family: his father, perhaps, but more importantly, his grandparents. I was nervous and excited as we walked holding hands, laughing at the children playing in the street."

Shelly is captivated by this beautiful love story, but she also wonders what happened, knowing that something sad is going to come of it all.

"I didn't even know Samuel's last name, not that it would have made any difference. I knew nothing of his family before that day. I had planned on telling Samuel about the pregnancy, but I never found the right time, thank God.

"I can still see his grandmother's face when she looked at me for the first time. She stared at me for the longest time before taking me into the dining room. As she regained her composure, she began asking questions about my family and me. I thought she was trying to ascertain if I was from a good enough family to be with her grandson. She asked who my mother was and when I was born. She seemed to be counting or adding in her head.

"She told Samuel and me to stay seated; she had something important to show us. I am so grateful Samuel told his family that I was a friend, because his grandmother brought out a picture of their daughter, who had died very young. Samuel's aunt—and mine too.

"She looked exactly like me, her hair, her eyes ... everything. It was as if we were identical twins. Born a generation apart, but twins just the same. Samuel turned white and I tried to keep breathing as his grandmother explained to us that we were half-siblings. Samuel's father was also mine."

Shelly drops the camera on the table next to her, and covers her mouth as she gasps. She can't believe what she is hearing.

"I suddenly felt like I was suffocating. The room became bright white and began to spin. I must have passed out, because when I woke up I was lying on Samuel's bed and a doctor was giving me an injection.

"I immediately thought of my mother. I jumped up and ran downstairs and out of the house as fast as my legs would carry me. Where was I going? What was I going to tell my mother? How could I tell anyone that the father of the child I was carrying is my brother?"

Shelly suddenly understands the meaning of *el Amor Imposible*. Until now, it had been an idea she came up with, something that seemed funny and ironic. Suddenly, the idea of an "impossible love" seems like a very serious thing. Now she understands that sadness that her Latino classmates felt at the end of *Romeo and Juliet*. She thinks to herself, *So Juan Jr.'s father is his uncle too. That is why it is such a big secret. Isabel, you deserve to have a beautiful life.* She can't explain her thought, though. Isabel has left her alone in the room.

Chapter 15

A touch of sunshine

One of the first things Shelly did when she began working at the Refugee Center was water the plants in the courtyard. Within weeks, the plants were growing and flowers were blooming. The courtyard no longer seemed like such a barren, depressing place. She also started bringing *atól* and tortillas, because she realized the women were not eating. The second week, she brought some of the neighborhood children with her and smiled when she heard them calling the women *Abuela*. Many of them had lost their grandparents or never knew them, so it was a perfect fit.

Shelly seems to have an intuitive understanding about human nature. She comprehends the idea that in order for humans to feel useful in this world, generations need to commingle. She understands that mothers and grandmothers need a reason to live, and that children feel better too, when they make an old person happy.

Despite all the sadness, the Refugee Center becomes a bustling little community. The women begin to bring presents to Shelly. Nothing extravagant, of course, but little trinkets: miniature pots and fruits made out of clay. Shelly doesn't feel right keeping them, so she has gotten Señor Gonzalez to make some shadow boxes to put the miniatures in. Shelly nails them up on the sparse and dingy walls. Soon new trinkets are being added every day. It gives the women something else to focus on, a touch of sunshine peeking into their dark lives.

Chapter 16

Intimate confession

Shelly tells Abuela that she needs to photograph her again. She looks surprised that Shelly would want to take more photos, so Shelly tells her the first ones didn't come out. The truth is that her image was stunning; you could see all her history in her face. Shelly wants more.

Once again, Abuela begins sharing her deepest secrets. "This world is so sad, mad, and confusing, and I'm supposed to act like everything is fine and normal for my family. I wish I could be like the young people and at least try to make a difference. I will spend my life being a mother, a grandmother, even a great-grandmother. I will spend my life feeling ashamed of the fact that I had a child out of wedlock while I act as if I am a devout Catholic. I know people talk behind my back. I go to church every day and try to be the best mother, daughter ... Catholic I can be, while all the time I am living a lie.

"Of course, the worst is that I lied to Isabel. She thinks her father is dead, when all these years he lived with his family just a few blocks from us. I am the worst kind of hypocrite."

This time Shelly lets Abuela talk and quietly takes photographs as Abuela tells her tales. She has all the animation of a trained theater actress, so there's no need to give her any direction.

"The day Isabel was born was the last day I ever spoke with her father. He saw her once and left. We were to be married in a few days but she was born early. I didn't think I was quite that far along. I never saw him again, never demanded an explanation. I was so embarrassed ... and so young. I guess I felt I didn't deserve to know what made him leave and never return."

Shelly is surprised to hear that this woman, who speaks her heart and mind to Shelly, could ever have been quiet and shy, and especially embarrassed.

"When Isabel was very small, I told her he was dead, and she never mentioned him again. She must have seen the distraught look on my face and decided to leave me alone in my grief."

Shelly feels guilty taking these photographs, as she realizes that the telling of the stories is making an impression on the photos. If she were to take the photos while Abuela sits quietly, they would not be the same, but Shelly is not forcing her to talk. She's not making Abuela tell her story. In fact, if she were to tell her not to talk, that she didn't want to hear it, she suspects Abuela would tell her anyway.

"The truth is that Isabel's father continued to live with his parents just seven blocks from my own parents' home. Isabel had another set of grandparents who had no interest in knowing her. Did Alberto convince them he was not the father? Is that what he believed? They say a grandmother knows whether a child came from their child, but they never even saw her, so they couldn't have made a judgment like that."

Shelly has stopped taking photos. This moment feels too personal, like it should not be intruded on, even by an inanimate object such as a camera. Shelly also hopes that no one comes home and ruins her chance of hearing completely this intimate confession. Yes, Shelly realizes, confession is exactly the right word. She remembers her mother teaching her about giving confession to the priest. She had told Shelly to tell him everything. "Everything bad you've ever done, Shelly. Don't hold back." At the time, Shelly was upset. She hadn't done anything bad. What could she say to this man in the fancy robes? Now, though, Shelly was beginning to see that confessing your sins could be very cleansing.

"Alberto *was* the father; this I know. To this day, he is the only man to know me in that way. No other man has seen the body underneath these clothes. He is the only man I ever loved. Of course, I will always love my new saint, San Romero, but that is a different, pure love. And I love God. That is the only thing that has kept me going all these years. Without my faith in God, who knows where I would have ended up?"

Shelly tries not to show her sadness at this statement. To have had such a short time to know love and spend the rest of your life without it seems unbearable to Shelly.

"Sometimes, I suspect Isabel knows the truth. Perhaps she has even met her paternal grandparents."

Shelly looks away when Abuela says this, in case her eyes give anything away. Maybe someday Isabel and her mother will have a heart-to-heart talk. Maybe someday Abuela will tell her the truth and Isabel can tell her mother that she *has* met that side of her family. But Shelly does not want to be—will not be—the one to tell Abuela the truth. Things will come out in their own time, in their own way. Shelly has to believe that.

"Of course, Isabel wouldn't tell me if she had met her paternal grandparents. She's afraid I couldn't handle it. She doesn't understand me, though. Enduring twenty years living so close to the father of my child makes one able to endure anything, anything except it happening to my own child. I could not handle seeing Isabel go through what I went through. Thank God she has Juan. He will always be there for her."

Shelly hopes this is true. Knowing that Señor Gonzalez was there for Isabel when she needed him most, when her unborn child needed a father, makes Shelly feel even closer to him. *What a good man he is*, Shelly thinks.

Chapter 17

Snippets from the past

Señor Gonzalez had told Shelly about his friend and *compañero*, Señor Martinez. He had spoken to her of his dedication and hard work, organizing unionists. He even organized protests and strikes. Though he also spoke of how educated Señor Martinez was, Shelly imagined him to be gruff and hard.

As they sit at the kitchen table talking, Shelly discovers Mr. Martinez to be a kind, soft-spoken, intelligent man. He knows a great deal about literature, especially Latin American literature. There is much Shelly could learn from him.

On this particular day, though, he seems determined to learn more about her. He asks, "Where in the US are you from?"

"Hilton, New York, is where my family lives, but I was born in Pennsylvania."

"And your parents?"

"My dad is from Ohio. I'm not sure about my mother. She may be from Kansas or Oklahoma or Arkansas. She never speaks about it, so I'm not sure."

"*¿Cual es tu apellido?*"

Shelly doesn't understand why he asks, as he knows her last name.

"Señor, you know my last name is Smith, the most common last name in the United States," Shelly says.

"*¿Si, pero, cual es el apellido de tu mamá?*" Shelly has forgotten that here, as in all of Latin America, children usually take both of their parents' last names. Shelly has always seen this as progressive, something they had over Americans, but she soon realizes that the mother's name is eventually dropped anyway. Two last names can be a bit cumbersome, but four, then eight ... well, it becomes impossible to continue after a generation or so. There are those who, for various reasons, choose to keep their mother's name, though, and not necessarily because they are illegitimate.

"My mother's maiden name is Dalton, *señor*, though I don't remember her mother's last name."

"Dalton, yes, I thought I could see a resemblance! How wonderful! You are half Salvadoran! You are one of us!"

He gets up from his chair and motions Shelly to stand up. He is hugging her with great vigor and is all smiles. *But what on earth ... is ... he ...? He couldn't think ...*

"Señorita, you are related to our country's greatest resource. You are a Dalton, granddaughter—okay, niece, yes, I believe you are the niece—of Roque Dalton, our greatest poet, our hero."

"Señor, I love the idea as much as you, but I don't think it could be true. My grandmother"—Shelly is getting confused herself now—"said my grandfather, Winnall, was killed." Her mind is racing now, trying to remember the snippets of conversations between her mother and the woman Shelly had always been told was her grandmother. Her great-grandmother spent the rest of her life in a depression after the loss of her son. When her great-grandma would start to tell Shelly about Grandpa Winnall, her mother would admonish her and tell her to keep quiet about something she knew nothing about. Shelly never could understand how her mother could talk to her own flesh and blood like that. But Shelly knew the truth now. Her grandmother had given her the beautiful tin box on her deathbed, the tin box that contained the letter Winnall wrote to his sister about having a son named Roque.

Yes, Shelly wanted it to be true more than anyone. She wanted to be related to Roque. If everything she had learned was true (and it did seem to be), Roque Dalton, El Salvador's most prolific and patriotic poet, was her uncle.

"Young lady," Señor Martinez tells her, "I'm going to prove it to you. You'll see."

Shelly wonders how he could know anything about her family. Or why he would even care. Except, she does know Roque Dalton's poetry. And she knows it is some of the most beautiful poetry she's ever read, even if she doesn't understand some of it.

Señor Martinez hugs Shelly again, then starts to shake hands with Mr. Gonzalez, but instead grabs him and gives him a bear hug. Then he's out the door. Shelly stands there wide-eyed, with her mouth open.

Chapter 18

Trust

The next day, Shelly hears a knock at the Gonzalezes' door. She opens the door to see that boy again, the boy of about ten years of age who keeps appearing when she least expects it. Shelly stares at him. He tells her, "You need to come with me," but won't say where.

Letty yells, "Who is it?"

"*Es el niño.*" Shelly yells. *The one who keeps showing up. The mystery boy.* She looks at the child. "*¿Cómo te llamas?*"

"Señorita, my name is Miguel."

Letty comes out from her room and looks at the boy.

"*Hola, Miguelito. ¿Qué tal?* Is everything okay?"

"*Si,* Niña Letty, but they told me to come and get *la norteamericana, la Chele.*"

Shelly is pacing the floor and she feels her blood pressure rise. *Who are 'they,' and why won't they say where 'they' want me to go?*

"*Está bién*, Miguelito. We'll be ready in a minute." Letty tells Shelly to put on her tennis shoes and grab a jacket.

"Letty, I need to know where we're going and why. Some boy can't just show up and tell us someone needs to see us and we drop everything," Shelly tells her. Her face is pink with anger. "Besides, I have work to do at ... they need me at ... the Refugee Center."

"Chele, *éste es importante*."

"How do you know it's more important?"

"*Confía en mi*, Chele," she tells her. And Shelly *does* trust her.

The next thing Shelly knows, she is walking with them up the mountain behind the houses. She decides to enjoy the walk, the air, and the exercise. It's been years since she hiked a mountain, so she is enjoying that sense of getting deeper into the woods—how the light changes, how it gets darker the further in you go, and how the smell of the earth and trees gets into your nostrils ... although she is still wondering where they are going and what they are going to do at the top of this mountain.

Miguelito and Letty are talking quietly, but Shelly is lost in her own world. She wonders why they're not following a trail. Miguelito seems to have them walking so as *not* to make a trail. Close to the top of the mountain, they come to a camp of some sort. Most of the people there are young. Shelly can tell by their old, ill-fitting clothes that they are poor, *campesinos*. A woman in fatigues approaches them, smiling. She grabs Shelly's hand.

"*Hola, soy Comandante Ana*."

"*Yo soy* Shelly."

Ana gives Shelly a hug.

"*Hola, compañera*," she says to Letty, and Shelly realizes that they know each other. Ana takes them around and introduces Shelly.

The kids come up to Letty and hug her, then very shyly hug Shelly too. They don't seem surprised or nervous that there's a *gringa* in their midst. As Ana tells Shelly the names of these kids, Letty explains that they are their *noms de guerre*. "No one uses their real names here."

From among all these brown-skinned people, out walks a handsome, blue-eyed, smiling gringo with beautiful, wild, dirty-blond hair. Ana says, "This is Comandante Carlos."

Shelly gasps and gulps and finally manages to get her hand out. "*Hola, soy* Shelly."

Shelly now understands the fascination people have with blue eyes. *They reflect your image back to you, which makes you feel like the person knows you and is totally focused on you.*

"We'll have to find a name for you before you come back again. It's a pleasure to finally meet you."

"What do you mean *finally*?"

"Lori got word to me that you were coming, and then that you had finally arrived."

"How? How did she do that?"

"Oh, we have our ways," Carlos answers.

Shelly looks at him, stunned.

As Carlos shows her around the camp, Letty goes off with Ana. Shelly cannot understand why Letty never mentioned her knowledge of the guerrillas and her agreement with their politics.

Carlos introduces Shelly to some of the boys, as young as Miguelito, some even younger. They are hiding their faces, though their eyes smile at her. *How bad could life in this country be, for children to be here fighting instead of out playing?* Shelly wonders.

Carlos tells her, "Most of them lost their parents in the war. They had no place to go. We try to find some kind of useful work for them because we all must do something to earn our right to be here."

"*¿Y ústed, Carlos? Qué hace ústed aquí?*" Shelly asks, suddenly embarrassed, not that she's speaking Spanish to this American, but that she dared to ask him what he does here to earn his keep. She realizes that she has been answering his English with Spanish.

Carlos doesn't answer her question, but he does answer Shelly's unspoken question: why? "Back in the US, I was studying law until I fell in love with history. Sadly, though, history is filled with injustice and inequality, the rape and murder of innocents. The victims being the noblest of society, won't fight back because they believe it is wrong to fight, to hurt another."

Shelly stares, not believing that this man is here, that he knows who she is, seems to know Lori, and that he could leave behind what sounds like a very good life to be here, putting his life in danger and wondering where his next meal will come from. Everyone here is skinny; the children look almost emaciated.

"Our country has often helped those who obtained power with might, illegally. I had to come to offset, in some small way, what our government is doing. I could not, in good conscience, continue with my beautiful life while my country allowed a cruel and unjust government to run roughshod over a people who just want to live ... and love."

Shelly listens quietly, not knowing what to say to Carlos or about this situation.

"These people want so little—a humble home with their entire family together. Instead the army comes and takes their land, insisting it was never theirs, that it always belonged to one of the fourteen families."

Shelly remembers her Central American history class. The professor talked about the fourteen families, the oligarchy that runs this country. He told the class they wouldn't find any reference to it in the history books, but if you go to El Salvador, you will hear about them, the people who own the country.

What Carlos is saying is correct, but she can't imagine going this far. She knows there are priests being killed, martyred. She's already witnessed the murder of Monsignor Romero. *But to take up arms against anyone, no matter how cruel, is going too far.*

As if reading her mind again, he continues. "Lori tells me you are a pacifist. I was a pacifist once. But how long can one sit on the sidelines and watch people being killed? How long can we wait while defenseless men, women, and even children are tortured? How many times can we look the other way and pretend not to know?

"You are going to hear horror stories of babies cut out of women's bellies, of men's heads being cut off and stuck on poles after their wives and daughters are raped in front of them. And they will all be true. This is what this government's army is doing to its own people."

Shelly cannot speak. She heard these stories before she came. That is why she is here, but being here, hearing this, not from a Salvadoran, but from an American not much older than she ... *that* she could never have imagined.

As Carlos and Shelly look out at San Salvador

below them, they can see all the shantytowns. Houses made of plywood, the reds, yellows, and greens of signs that make up many of the shacks. Carlos tells her, "You are here because we have a job that needs to be done. You are the only one who can do it; otherwise we wouldn't ask."

"But ... I don't understand. How do you even know anything about me? I am just some crazy American coming here thinking I can somehow make a difference."

"Yes, that is what Lori's message said, that you were a very good person, though she did say you were rather naive."

"The more you talk, the more confused I get. How do you know Lori?"

"Lori is my wife. And Tina is my daughter. When I told Lori I was coming here, it was only with her agreement to keep news coming back and forth."

Shelly is quiet now, looking straight ahead. She can't imagine anyone giving up a family to come do this. *And why didn't Lori tell me? She didn't think I could be trusted?*

Carlos, seeming to read her mind again, says, "She couldn't tell you and take the chance that something might slip out of your mouth—inadvertently, of course. She knew you were trustworthy, but ..."

But what? Shelly wonders. *I am trustworthy but can't be trusted to know why I was offered this opportunity to come here?*

"As I was saying, there is a twenty-nine-year-old journalist, Mayra Rodriguez Silva, who has been in prison for more than a year now. She is being tortured, beaten, kept in isolation. She has been charged with crimes against the government, treason. Because of her work, you and I and many others know about the war. For years, it was El Salvador's best kept secret."

Shelly shifts nervously, and he continues.

"They will probably kill her. Lori gave you a package to deliver. Do you remember?" Shelly stares at him and doesn't say a word. "Well, you don't have to deliver it. You just have to smuggle it into the prison and take some photographs of Mayra before she is killed. The world must see what our government's money has paid for in this country."

Shelly stands there ... looking out at San Salvador, ignoring Carlos. She can't believe this complete stranger is asking her to risk her life for him. *What gives him the right?* she asks herself. She feels her blood running hot with anger.

"Before you say no, go see her. While you are there, you can scope things out. If after talking to her, you decide you can't or won't do it, we will understand. Not everyone is cut out for this kind of work."

Shelly cannot speak and is suddenly flushed. She feels the urge to run. Carlos must see this. His look seems to say, *I wouldn't ask if I didn't have to.*

"We have no one else we can ask, *compañera.* The few foreign journalists who haven't left or been killed are being followed twenty-four hours a day. They couldn't get away with taking the photos, let alone get them out of the country."

"I ... must ... go now," Shelly manages to say. She turns and begins walking quickly down the mountain without saying anything, not to Letty, and not to their guide, Miguelito. Tears are streaming down her face. Shelly wonders how Lori could do this to her. She trusted her! It occurs to Shelly that Lori had to have had this in mind all along. She thought they had become friends, but now it seems to Shelly that Lori was just using her. Shelly thought she could trust Lori. She thought she could trust all these people. Now she wonders what on earth she is doing here.

Chapter 19

Just in case

Although Shelly is walking fast, Letty and Miguelito catch up to her. They walk back for some time in silence.

Suddenly Miguelito says, "Señorita Chele, they told me to give this to you."

Shelly takes the heavy object wrapped in a scarf, and unwraps it.

"A gun! What is wrong with these people?"

"Dijeron qué es para su protección, señorita."

"Protection? I don't need protection! From what? I do not want this! I will never use this, no matter what is happening! I would rather die than hurt someone else. I would rather be killed than kill," Shelly cries out, seeing in her mind the beautiful deer falling, blood flowing down its slick brown fur.

Letty takes it from Shelly's hands and says calmly, "I have a place for it. Don't worry about it."

When they arrive at the house, Letty tells Shelly to watch her *just in case*. "Just in case you should need to use it. There is a little opening here, to allow a worker to crawl under the house." Letty pulls the frame out and places the gun where it can easily be grabbed. She tells Shelly, "We know where it is if something terrible were to happen. Hopefully, two or three years from now, I'll remember it's there and get rid of it. Hopefully we will never need it."

Shelly wants to be angry at Letty, along with all the others, but she can't. Shelly is beginning to see the reality: children fighting, mothers fighting, an educated American giving up everything to come here to fight, leaving behind a wife and child that he loves. Shelly remembers Lori working day and night, trying to get the word out to people. Carlos and Lori could be having an idyllic life, ignoring what is happening here. Instead they are separated from each other and Carlos is separated from his child, not knowing whether they'll ever see each other again. Shelly wonders how much Lori has thought about that, how she would deal with losing her husband.

Letty enters. "Where is the camera, Chele?"

"I'm so sorry, Letty. I hid it under the mattress ... until I figured out what I was to do with it." She pulls the fake watch—obviously too big to be what it pretends to be—out from under the mattress, by the wall.

"It's okay," Letty says soothingly. She takes Shelly's hands in her own. "Just go and see the woman. You'll know what to do after that. If you decide not to do it, I know someone who can use the camera."

Shelly lies down. She is thinking about home. She remembers her mother telling her, "It's okay. Shelly, you'll know what to do."

Shelly dreamed of her mother all night and awoke with a sense of calm that she had never felt before.

Chapter 20

Little soldier

The next morning, Shelly wakes up knowing she needs to call her mother. She gently shakes Letty awake and asks, "Can you take me to the store so I can call home? I'm afraid if I go alone, I'll get disconnected before I finish the call."

"*Pues si*, of course I can go with you. Just give me a couple minutes to dress. We can grab something to eat there."

When they arrive at the store, Shelly's palms begin to sweat. They walk in and go straight to the phone. Letty gets ten *colones* in change, so Shelly will have plenty of time to talk.

Shelly slowly dials the number, but then finds herself hoping that her mother is not home. *Not much chance of that, though. She almost never leaves the house.* Shelly's dad buys the groceries and her mom does her socializing at home. The phone rings three, then four times ... maybe it's Shelly's lucky day. Then, bbrrrriiinnngg ... "Hello, Smith residence, Mrs. Smith speaking." She is breathing heavily.

"Mom, it's me. I can't believe you still answer the phone that way, with three of your kids no longer living at home."

"Well, how do I know if it's one of my children or a bill collector?" she says, sounding peeved that Shelly would question her etiquette.

"What were you doing? Playing hanky-panky with Dad? You're all out of breath."

"Hush! You know those operators listen in on the conversations!"

"Mom, that was back in the old days when the operator had to connect each individual call. And even then, I doubt they had the time or the inkling to listen to our boring conversations," Shelly tells her.

"Enough about telephone conventions. You don't call from that far away for that. How are you, honey? Are you coming home soon?"

She always asks that same question, Shelly thinks.

"No, Mom. Like I told you when I left, I'm going to El Salvador and I don't know when I'll be back home. And now I'm here."

"Honey, if you need money, we can send you enough to get home and back so you can be here for Christmas."

This is why I don't call home more often. It's like listening to a broken record. Shelly wonders how her father has put up with her all these years.

"Anyway, Mom, I'm doing fine. Thanks for asking. How's everyone over there?"

"Oh, honey, I know you're doing fine. You're our little soldier. You're always doing fine. Everyone is good here ... except ... well ... your brother, he lost his job."

"Tommy lost his job?"

"No, sweetheart, when have you ever known Tommy to lose a job? Billy lost his job at the factory. They're talking about moving down south. Or even

Mexico."

"Billy wants to move to Mexico?"

"No, honey, the company might move to Mexico. They're trying to get everyone to take a cut in pay so they're threatening to move. Jeez, I sure wish you were here. We don't ever have this much trouble communicating when you're here, at home."

"Mom, we always have this much trouble communicating."

Sometimes I swear she does this on purpose, just to keep the conversation from getting too deep. Shelly remembers how she always wanted conversations to be nice and light. She couldn't even talk politics in the house. Shelly and her dad had to go fishing in order to have a discussion of any substance.

"Shelly, if you need money, you know all you have to do is ask."

"No, Mom, I don't need money. Remember, that's why I went to New Orleans first, to earn enough for my stay in El Salvador?"

"Okay, but if you need any, you know you can come to us, right?"

She's going to drive me crazy, I swear.

"Shelly, I found the tin box that your grandmother left you. I read the letters."

"Mom, those were mine! You had no right!"

"Okay, I'm sorry, but the woman was my mother. Or at least, that's what I thought. Please believe me, if I had known the truth, I would have told you. I had no idea. I mean, your grandmother ... Shelly, she will always be your grandmother--"

"Yes, she will, but Mom, this is very important. We

can't talk about this now, not while I am here."

"But Shelly, I am trying to tell you that it's okay. You were right. I should have known, and I should have told you about Winnall ... but honestly––"

"Mother, if you don't stop, I'm going to have to hang up. This cannot be discussed while I am here. You have to trust me. It is a matter of life and death."

"Oh, you're always so dramatic."

"I am begging you to stop. When I get home, we can talk all about this, but we can't talk about it now. I have to hang up now. Maybe someone else can explain it to you. This cannot be discussed again, not until I get home. Mother, I love you. Now ... goodbye."

She hears her mother sobbing, and she wishes she could comfort her, but if anyone hears the name *Dalton* in relation to her, she may never see her mother again. She may be sent home in a body bag. Of course, Shelly knows it is her own fault that her mother doesn't understand. She had pretended like coming here was some extended vacation; she hadn't wanted her mother to worry about her.

Shelly is finally beginning to understand her mother. She was traumatized by seeing her own mother and grandmother so upset, and as a small child could only try to comfort the two people she loved most. For this reason, she has always tried to keep her own children from having intense discussions or feeling disturbing emotions. She's only been trying to control the environment of her loved ones the way she couldn't, as a child.

Letty is trying to catch up to Shelly. Shelly knows she wants an explanation, but she can't decide what to tell her, so she yells, "Sorry, I have to get to the center. I should have been there an hour ago!"

Chapter 21

Old friends

Shelly has been bugging Abuela for some time to take her to meet Paula, the woman who gave birth to Mr. Gonzalez. Shelly isn't sure, but she suspects that Paula was the daughter of Don Pablito and Doña Consuelo, the couple who worked for Don Fernando. She hates using *Don* for that man—he deserves no one's respect—but that is what Abuela calls him, so Shelly does too. If Shelly's recollections are right, Don Fernando ordered the killing of Paula's parents. She wonders if he had his eyes on her and that is why he killed them. Maybe the peasant uprising had nothing to do with his decision. Either way, she hopes she never sees that evil man again. *Abuela may have forgiven him, but I cannot.*

"Let's go, Chele. Don Fernando is in the hospital so Paula is at the house alone."

"Thank you, Abuela. Did you tell her I want to photograph her?"

"No, *amor*, she is a humble woman. She would never let you come if she thought that you were going to photograph her. I told her you have never tasted quesadilla, our Salvadoran cheesecake. She said you must come try it. She knows that hers is the best, as many of the neighbors buy it from her rather than having their own *criadas* make it."

"*¿Criada?* They call her a maid?"

"No, Chele, I am just making the point that she makes it better than the maids who are trained to make it. It is a way for her to have her own money. She is too embarrassed to ask Don Fernando. Chele, she *was* the family maid for many years."

"But now she is the mother of his child."

"Chele, *ten cuidado*. Don't say anything about that to her."

"But, Abuela, what happens if the old man dies? Where will she go?"

"Well, I know his sons will show up then and try to get everything. I don't know what will happen to her. Maybe Juan Sr. will finally act like a son to her."

Shelly still can't imagine that Señor Gonzalez, the kindest man she's ever met, could abandon his mother like that.

"I sure hope so."

"*Niña*, that's why I love you so much. You haven't even met her, and you already care about her."

"Abuela, I promise not to say anything that would embarrass her."

"*Si*, I know, *mi amor*." Abuela gives her another hug before she knocks on the door. "Hopefully she remembers we are coming," she says softly. Paula opens the door, smiling despite herself. "*Hola*, Paula. *Cómo has estado*?"

"Come in, Maria Elizabeth. Come in, *niña bonita*." Shelly blushes. She still can't get used to everyone noticing her beauty. Shelly offers her hand, and Paula gives her a limp handshake. Unlike most Salvadorans, she is too self-conscious to hug her. *I hope I never see that old man again. I hope he dies!* Shelly immediately realizes what she has thought and asks God to forgive her.

"*Ven*, come sit here in the kitchen." Abuela had told Shelly she would take them into the kitchen. It is the only room she feels is hers in the huge mansion. Shelly had asked her where Paula slept, but Abuela said she would never ask her such a question.

Paula gives them *café con leche* and brings out a big plate of *quesadilla*. This Salvadoran cheesecake is made with cornmeal so it has a different texture than American-style cheesecake. She puts down little plates and cloth napkins. *We are her special guests. What a sweet lady she is.* Of course, Shelly knows very little about her, but she likes her all the same.

Finally, Paula sits down with her own cup of black coffee. She has given them milk, but doesn't take it for herself. "Paula, put some *leche* in your coffee too. It will give you strength," Abuela tells her.

"Ay, Maeli, I am so used to my coffee like this, it doesn't taste right to me with milk."

Shelly realizes that these two are old friends. *Probably the only real friend Paula has ever had.* Shelly takes a small piece of the cake. "Oh my, this is delicious! *Muy rica, Señora!*"

Paula blushes. "Thank you, *niña*. You are a darling."

Well, at least I'm not the only one blushing around here.

"So, Maeli says you are getting very close to my grandchildren. Tell me what they are like."

"Oh, Letty is a smart girl and very kind, but I will have to get back to you about Juan Jr. He's a bit complicated. He is very polite, but that's about all I know for sure." Shelly laughs and Paula smiles, happy to hear anything about the family she never sees.

The two women are talking so fast Shelly can hardly keep up. Plus, they are mostly talking about people from their childhood, so Shelly asks if it is okay to look around. Who knows when she'll have another chance to see what a rich Salvadoran lives like? She wanders through the rooms, looking at the beautiful mahogany furniture and the paintings on the walls. *Real paintings, not just prints*. This place could be made into a museum. It smells musty, but Shelly even enjoys that. It takes her back to the farm, the place her dad grew up. And where she had spent her early childhood.

Shelly notices some old photographs on the other wall. She walks over and looks at them for a long time. Pictures of Don Fernando's grandfather.

A daguerreotype—the first photographs ever made. Next she sees a very old picture of a christening. She remembers the pictures of her own christening. She was just a baby.

Shelly remembers the arguments her parents had about it. Her mother: "But you agreed to the baptism, Thomas." Her dad: "Yeah, I agreed. After you cried for a week, I began to think you would never stop crying if I didn't let you baptize my girl." Her mother: "So I am going to have to cry again, so you will let me take her to church on Sundays?" Her dad: "No, guess what? If she wants to go, you can take her. If she doesn't, you can't."

It occurs to Shelly she only said no because she

knew her dad wanted her to. She broke her mother's heart just so she could feel closer to him. *Oh, Mom, I am so sorry.*

"Chele, time to go. *¿Chele, vos estás bién?*"

"Huh, uh, yeah, I'm okay. I was looking at the beautiful photos."

"Paula, *nos vemos muy pronto*, okay?"

"But Abuela, we forgot to ask her about letting me take some photos."

"Paula, *Chele esta haciendo fotos de todos nosotros.* She will make you look beautiful. You'll see."

"*La próxima vez*, yes? Next time you come visit, okay?" Paula says.

She knows we probably won't be back. That's why she is agreeing to it.

"Yes, thank you, Señora Paula."

"Paula. Just call me Paula."

On the walk home, Shelly considers whether she should tell Abuela her secret, that she was baptized, but chose not to go to church, just to please her father. She supposes she also did it so she could spend time alone with her dad. *He let her christen the rest of the children and they all went with mother to church.*

Chapter 22

Native tongue

Shelly's heart is pounding as she sees him up ahead. Not that she has any idea who he is, but she knows for sure that he is American. She looks around at the bombed-out buildings and spots a place to hide, but before she can get there the children start shouting *"¡Ita Chele, Ita Chele!"* They all come running over to her; one of them is carrying a soccer ball, the one she brought them from the United States.

The young man calmly walks toward her, smiling. He is not in uniform, but his haircut and stance give him away.

"American, right?"

"Maybe, maybe not," Shelly responds.

"Well, if you were Canadian, you would have said so immediately."

"So, maybe I'm British, or Australian."

"No, I don't detect any accent."

"So, what? What if I am American?"

"Hah, so you are! William H. Masterson, at your service."

"Hah, and I knew you were military."

"Oh, you did, huh? And how did you know that?"

"Oh, come on."

"Is it that obvious?"

"Yes, sir, it is."

"You don't have to call me *sir*. William is fine. Or

Will. Or Bill."

"Who says I want to call you anything?" Shelly realizes that it seems like she is flirting, but she is stalling, trying to come up with a viable story to explain what the hell she is doing in this war-torn country.

"Okay, Bill it is, cuz you remind me of my sister."

"Look, I'm not looking for a friend—"

"Not looking, but you found one anyway. So, come on, tell me your name. Please?"

"I'm serious. This ... this won't look right." Shelly's face is scrunched up. Now she's said too much.

"Won't look right to who?"

"The Salvadorans. They get nervous when they see soldiers." She knows she is only digging herself deeper.

"They called you *Ita Chele*. Is that your name? Ita?"

"No, of course not. Ita is short for Señorita. Okay, look, my name is Shelly, but that's all I'm going to tell you."

"Alright, now we're getting somewhere. So, Shelly, what part of the States are you from?"

"I didn't say I was American."

"No, but you are."

Shelly blurts out, "Kansas," before she can think. Her grandfather had been in Kansas when he got in trouble with the law.

"Uh-huh, Kansas is a state. Where in Kansas?"

"Nowhere. I mean, you never heard of it." The more Shelly talks, the worse it gets. All she knows is that her grandfather fled Kansas and that's how he ended up here.

"Alright, don't worry about it. How 'bout we get

some food and talk a little?"

"No, I can't. I'm on my way to ... work." Shelly's face is scrunched up with worry now.

"Wow, you get more interesting by the second. You have a job? Here, in El Salvador?"

"No, it's not a real job. I mean, I'm not doing anything illegal."

"Whoa, hold on. Look, just 'cuz I'm in the military doesn't mean I'm looking to arrest anyone."

"Hah, I got you to admit something."

"Well, no use denying it. You said it was obvious."

"Look, I'm here as a photographer. A *portrait* photographer. I can't be seen with you."

"Okay, let's meet up later."

Against Shelly's better judgment, she agrees. She only now realizes how much she misses her native tongue. Besides, maybe she can find out more about the US presence here.

"Mariscos del Mar, five o'clock, okay?"

"Yeah, okay. I gotta go now. See you then."

Shelly quickly walks away, but finds herself wondering if she has just made a huge mistake. *Oh well, I guess I could just not show up. It's not like he's going to come find me.* At least, she hopes not.

Chapter 23

Guns and black beans

Shelly works quietly, wondering if she should meet Bill or not. Between photos, she waters the plants and adds miniatures to the shadow boxes that Señor Gonzalez made for Shelly's gifts from the women. Shelly smiles when she hears the women talking to each other and getting quite lively when the children pop in to say hi and get a much needed hug ... or two.

"Ceci, I met an American—"

"Pardon, Shelly, I couldn't hear you with all this racket." Ceci is smiling too.

"Oh, never mind." Shelly is relieved that she didn't hear her. *No one can say I didn't try to mention it to someone.*

As Shelly runs out of the center, she notices a cab so she flags it down. *Might as well, since I'm late. I'll just go fancy all the way.*

Shelly looks back to see the children waving. Her face is red, but she waves back at them, not sure why she should be embarrassed.

The cabby tries to converse with her in broken English. Shelly pretends she doesn't speak Spanish. She has noticed that some of the less educated men think she is flirting with them when she speaks to them in their native language. Besides, her mind is on what to tell Bill, and what not to tell him. She knows she shouldn't reveal too much.

Bill is sitting in a chair outside the restaurant. He runs over to say, "Shelly, keep your money. I got this."

"No, I can't let you do that."

"Yes, you can. You know when was the last time I ran into an American while out of country?"

"No, how could I--?"

"Never. Besides, if I spend money on you, it's less I'll have to waste on booze."

Shelly stares at him.

"Hah, I got you again. I drink one beer a day, two tops."

Shelly's heart is racing, but she doesn't know why.

Once inside, Bill orders *ceviche de conchas*, a Salvadoran dish of lemon-marinated mussels that Shelly has discovered does not upset her stomach. Well, except for the time she ate it at the beach. The water must have been polluted because she threw up everything she had eaten that day. Bill also orders lobster and shrimp, as well as beans, rice, and *curtido* (the same marinated cabbage that comes with the *pupusas*). Shelly is relieved, as she can eat much of what Bill has ordered.

"I am a vegetarian, but seafood doesn't bother me too much."

"Are you kidding? With all the great meat dishes they make here? Isn't it difficult?"

"Not if you're poor. But yes, the middle class eats a lot of meat, especially if they have guests."

"Why don't you eat meat?"

"It's a long story, but it has to do with shooting a deer, yet not killing it. I had to watch it die."

"Who killed it?"

"Believe it or not, I did. But that was the first and last time I shot a sentient being."

"So, do all the girls in Nowhere Town, Kansas, shoot guns?"

"No, just me. And that was a mistake."

As the food arrives, Bill begins eating. Shelly puts the black beans and rice on her plate and mixes them together. "Do you like *casamiento*? Marriage?"

"That's what that means? I am getting used to it."

"I love it," Shelly says as she puts a spoonful into her mouth.

"So, tell me again what *you* are doing here. Taking photos, you say."

"Yes, I take photos of regular Salvadorans. Some churches are paying for me to be here working on this project." Shelly again wonders if she is saying too much. She decides not to mention the Refugee Center. She doesn't want him coming back there ... to look for her.

"Regular people in the middle of a war. Hmmm."

"Yeah, there's a lot of history in people's faces. Besides, it's fun. My turn. What are you doing here?"

"Well, mostly it's classified so I can't tell you, but I train people."

"Soldiers, you mean?"

"I can't say."

"Classified?"

"Yeah, but I can say that I'm a CO."

"CO?"

"Commanding officer. But officially I am an advisor. You know, one of those fifty that Congress is allowing here."

"Well, I remember something about that. They don't want our soldiers fighting *their* war."

"Yeah, that is the gist of it. I just do what I am told."

"Yeah, don't question. Just do."

"That's how it works in the ... ah, military."

"I hope you're realizing what good people the Salvadorans are."

"Yes, very kind, gentle people. It's too bad Cuba and the Soviet Union are ruining things here."

Shelly stops chewing, sets down her fork, and stares at Bill. "You have got to be kidding ... right?"

"No, this is not a joking matter."

"Where did you get such an idea?"

"The CIA has documented the involvement of Cuba and the USSR."

"How could they even get into this country?"

"There are many ways in."

"This is an indigenous struggle. There is a long history of oppression by the army and the government, of generals becoming presidents. You do know about 1932, right?"

"We are trained extensively before we go into a country. The Communists have been here for fifty years; you are right about that."

"Yeah, this is all the fault of the Communists. Where do they get their weapons, then?"

"Like I said, Cuba and the Soviet Union."

"Bill, come on. I heard they are the same weapons used in Vietnam."

"The soldiers' weapons, that's right."

Shelly stands up quickly, knocking over the chair.

"I gotta go ... This was a huge mistake."

"Shelly, stop. Can't we discuss this as civil human beings? Civil Americans? That's why I do this. So you and I can speak our mind."

"No, we can't, because you don't know what you're talking about. And yeah, so we Americans can speak our mind, but not the rest of the world, right?"

Bill is following Shelly out of the restaurant. Everyone is staring at them.

"What about the massacres? *El Mozote? Rio Lempa?*"

"The army massacred guerrillas and the guerrillas massacred civilians."

Shelly gasps and stares, eyes wide, then runs to the street yelling, *"Taxista!"* She jumps into the first taxi, not caring that it is rusty, dented, and has bullet holes in the door. *"Por favor, váyase rápido!"*

Chapter 24

Not very happy

As Shelly relates the story of Bill to Letty, she looks at her with unsympathetic eyes. "Chele, how could you be so *ingenua*? Does he know where we live? Or where you work?"

"Letty, no, he doesn't. I mean he could find the center 'cuz I ran into him there, but no, he has no idea where we live."

"Well, you better let Ceci know not to give out any information. At least my brother is good for something. If he does find us, we can have Juan Jr. talk to him." Shelly breathes a sigh of relief. "Shelly, how could you think this could be okay?"

"Well, Abuela said that the soldiers just didn't know the truth."

"Abuela? Are you kidding me? She knows nothing about the war."

"Well, you would be surprised what she knows. And John told us about the soldiers who enlist right out of high school."

"But you said he—"

"I know. He's a commanding officer. It was really stupid of me, Letty. I see that now."

"Alright, Chele, probably nothing will come of this, but please—if you see any other Americans, stay away!"

"What about Carlos?"

"Chele, stop. *Híjole*, are you sure you're twenty-four years old? *Dios mio.*"

"Twenty-five next month," Shelly says, trying to lighten the mood.

"Well, sometimes I would swear you are a silly *adolecente*."

Shelly plops down on the bed and before she puts her skinny pillow over her face, shouts, "Close the door! And don't tell anyone I'm here."

Letty pushes the door, not meaning to slam it, but it does slam, making a loud bang, but just before it closes, Shelly looks up in time to see Abuela sneaking into the house. *"Hola, mi amor. ¿Dónde está la Chelita?"*

"Shhh, Abuela. She's in our room, but she's not very happy right now..."

"That's okay. I'll cook her something to cheer her up."

Chapter 25

Of love and orphans

Letty has told Shelly to meet her at school today. She said she wanted Shelly to meet someone very special to her. The way Letty went on and on about this young man, Shelly suspects she may be in love with him, but she kept quiet and let Letty tell her all about him.

Shelly waits outside Letty's classroom for her. She gets very concerned watching Letty trying to manage without books when everyone else has one. *Why hasn't she mentioned this to me? I would have bought the books she needed. That's what the money the church groups send every month is for,* Shelly thinks. *For necessities, and this certainly is a necessity.*

When Letty comes out, Shelly insists on taking her to a *pupuseria* two blocks from the school. She'd passed it on the way from the Refugee Center. "We just have to try it."

"*Está bién.* It's one of my favorite places," Letty tells her.

They order *pupusas*, of course, since that's all they sell. But Shelly isn't talking. She'd been so excited about taking Letty to eat here when she passed it on the way to pick her up. But now, sitting in the *pupuseria*, Shelly looks sadly at Letty. *Why didn't she tell me about her struggles in school?*

"Letty, why don't you have a math book? Everyone

else in the class has one."

"Oh, Chele, don't worry. It's one of the challenges I must overcome. It will make me stronger, having to figure out how to manage without books. *No tengo libros para ninguna de mis clases.*"

"*¿Porqué?* Why don't you have any books?"

"Because each book cost about twenty-five *colones* and we don't have that kind of money."

"I have the money. I can give it to you today."

"No, Chele, it wouldn't be right. I could not take your money."

"What? Why not?"

"*Mira*, you are here to help my people."

"Exactly. And helping you would help them, in the long run."

"*Vos no sabés eso.* I could finish medical school and move to the US and make tons of money. I could use you, Chele."

"First of all, you wouldn't do that—"

"How can you be so sure?"

"Second of all, it's not that simple. A medical degree from here does not just transfer over in the US. You would have to start your studies all over again *in English.*" Shelly knows this because Manuel, Victor's brother, had tried to finish his studies in the US. He ended up back in El Salvador because he would have had to apply to medical school there and start his studies all over again. Then there's the issue of knowing enough English. Neither of them had that good a handle on English.

"I will not take your money. I cannot do that in good conscience. Thank you though, *por tener tanta confianza en mi.*"

"Of course, I trust you and I believe in you."

"Chele, the answer is no."

It is obvious that Letty is not going to change her mind so Shelly focuses on eating her *pupusas*. It is hard to enjoy this, the most popular Salvadoran food, after their conversation; she is even more frustrated than before. This discussion proves that Letty deserves the help, that she would use it wisely, yet she won't accept it.

"Forget about all that stuff. There's someone special you're going to meet today. As soon as we finish, I'm going to take you there." Letty seems relieved to have changed the subject to something that to Shelly seems less personal. She adds, "Chele, you are a good person, but you don't understand us. There are people who need help *now*. That's who you should focus on."

"It looks like you're not giving me any choice in the matter."

"Besides, if you keep it up, I'm going to make you tell me why you were so mean to your mother. I'll make you tell me why you hung up the phone on her."

"Letty, I will tell you why. Just not today, not while we are out in public where it could be overheard. *¿Oís?*"

"Alright, Chelita, another time, we will talk about it. But, don't think I am going to forget about it."

Shelly insists on paying, and since Letty barely has enough money to cover lunch for the rest of the week, she lets her.

As they head toward the orphanage, Letty tells

Shelly about the person she is going to meet. She doesn't mention his name, but does tell her how he is helping the orphans here in San Salvador, and how he is studying medicine and––

"Letty, are you in love with *éste muchacho*? Please, tell me. I can hardly stand the suspense."

"Chele! No, it's not like that. He's just a really good person, that's all. Besides, he is considering becoming a priest, so no, I am not in love with him."

But Shelly can tell that she's lying.

"Okay, if you say so. So how old is he?"

"Twenty-two, I think. Something like that."

"And how long have you known him?"

"A few years ... well, a couple years, ever since he got back. I mean, I met him before he left. Miguelito introduced us, so I could get the medical stuff, you know?" Letty is practically whispering. She shouldn't be talking about this at all.

As Letty leads her to her secret friend, Shelly notices that the neighborhoods are getting more and more dilapidated. In the distance, she sees the shantytown homes that Victor had told her about— houses made of tin, scrap wood, and even cardboard, whatever people could find at the dumps or the side of the road. Shelly sees women carrying plastic tubs on their heads, coming back from a day of selling tortillas or whatever else they could scrape together to sell. There are also women carrying water jugs back to their home. *What a sad scene*. Though it occurs to Shelly that she could take some great photos here.

"*Estamos casi alli*, Chele, just a couple more blocks. You've never been here before, huh? Just remember, Chele, someday things will be better. Someday everyone will have a home." Letty winks at Shelly and smiles. "Someday all children will go to school."

She has so much optimism. I sure hope she's right.

"Letty, shhhh, someone might hear you."

"Don't worry. The army doesn't come here. They are afraid of these people. They have nothing left to lose, so they are certain that they're all *vos sabés que.*"

Shelly knows exactly what Letty means: *They think they're all guerrillas.*

They walk up to a gated area. Shelly sees a small building with a cross in front, and Miguelito answers Letty's shouts by running up and opening the gate. As soon as they enter, they are surrounded by children. The children smile shyly; some are shouting "Hola!" and the little ones are hiding behind the bigger ones, but it is obvious that they all want to be noticed. They must always be hoping and praying that *this* visitor will take them home.

Letty pulls Shelly through the swarm of children as she asks each one their name. "We could be here all day and miss the opportunity for you to meet my friend," Letty complains.

Father Buenpastor comes out smiling, with his *arms open wide. "¡Hola, mis amigas! ¿Cómo les vá?"*

"Hola, padre, muy bien. Quiero presentarle mi amiga Noorteamericana, Chele."

Shelly gives her hand to the padre. He shakes it, then gives her a big hug. She accepts it timidly, just as she did with Letty's family the day they met her. But she is smiling; she is happy to be here around all these children.

"*Mucho gusto, Padre*. Letty has been talking about you and your work for days." Shelly looks at Letty as if she is asking, "Why didn't you tell me?" Letty laughs. Shelly thinks this is the man Letty's been telling her about. Since Letty forgot to mention the padre, her confusion is understandable.

"We all do what we can, Chele. It's a pleasure for the children just to have visitors, so thank you for coming. Come inside. Do you have time for a five-minute tour?"

Shelly notices Letty's sudden smile and looks in the direction of her gaze. With the sunlight shining behind him, he looks like an angel.

"Manuel!" Shelly shouts, while Letty simply stares as Shelly runs over and hugs the young man Letty has been talking about since the day Shelly won over her trust. "Oh my God, I never thought I would see you here. There was so much to do before I came, I forgot to ask Victor how to contact you."

"So much for the surprise," Letty tells them both, "It seems you two are already acquainted."

"Oh no, this is a wonderful surprise. It's so funny that you never mentioned Chele's name. I would have known it was her immediately! Well, Letty, this is how God works. Look at how he has brought us all together." Manuel looks so happy; he's hugging Letty and Shelly, smiling and laughing.

"Look at how jubilant the children are. It is so important for them to see joy, for them to remember what happiness is," the priest says, noting that Manuel cannot contain his joy.

While Manuel shows Shelly around, he explains to Letty about his brother and New Orleans.

"But, Manuel, you never told me you had a brother," she exclaims.

"No, Letty, I have many things to tell you when the time is right." Whatever he means by that, Letty seems to have no idea. Shelly imagines it means the two of them will be spending more time together, so when Letty smiles, Shelly smiles too. As they look around at the children's barracks—one for the boys and one for the girls—Shelly thinks about Victor and how she came to meet the two Salvadorans in New Orleans. She wonders how he is doing.

Shelly suddenly realizes that she seems to have the power to read minds. She swears she sees Letty breathing a sigh of relief, glad that she didn't tell her more. Shelly is quite sure that Letty is in love with Manuel and that Manuel loves her back. She smiles for them both. And keeps on smiling, realizing that they may someday help these orphans find a home.

Chapter 26

A promise

As Manuel watches Shelly walk down the steps of the bus, he waves her down.

"Why didn't you call a taxi? We Salvadorans are used to our old, smelly buses, but I'm sure you brought enough money to get around in a little more style than that."

"Uh, hi. Nice to see you, too." Shelly smiles.

"*Perdonáme*, Chele. *Es un placer siempre* to see you again. In my concerns for your safety, I have forgotten my manners."

"Manuel, it's okay. I was just giving you a hard time." This time, Shelly does the hugging. She is smiling like she is the one in love. She never imagined she would ever see this courageous young man again.

"Shelly, I don't want to scare you, but it isn't safe for anyone who looks like they have money to be riding the buses. A blonde, green-eyed *norteamericana* obviously has money." Manuel continues to hug Shelly, looking at her and smiling.

"Well, this is one time they would be mistaken. I never carry more than twenty *colones* on me. That was one of the first things the Gonzalezes taught me," Shelly tells him, knowing he wants to hear about his brother. She hopes he won't be disappointed with what she has to say, which isn't much. Victor had gotten very distant once Shelly made up her mind that she was leaving, that she was going to El Salvador no matter what he said to try to change her mind.

When they'd met yesterday, Manuel had invited Shelly to meet him at *Hospital Bloom* today. Shelly was happy to say yes, not just to go to the children's hospital, but also to spend some time with a friend, a friend she knew from the States.

"Manuel, I didn't come here to find out how the rich live. I am here to experience life like a Salvadoran. Besides, I like riding the bus. Everyone is kind and ... well, I just like watching the people, seeing how people manage here. If I had my way, I would be taking pictures of them. Then you all would really be complaining!"

"It's lunchtime for me. Do you want to go eat before we go into the hospital?"

"Yes, of course. I am starving," Shelly cringes after she hears herself. *I will never use that term so loosely again.*

They walk to a little corner restaurant, what they would call a food stand in the US, but Shelly smiles as she looks at the three little tables on the broken sidewalk. "They don't have menus. I hope you don't mind."

Shelly says, "Manuel, I don't think I've seen a menu since I got here!" They both laugh.

"*¿Hola, Ita Lili, qué tal?*" Manuel says to the woman taking orders. "I eat here almost every day since I got back, so I know the cook ... cashier ... owner. "Ita Lili does it all."

"*Bien, bien, Manuelito. Y vos?*"

"What have you made today *para mi y mi amiga*? *¿Cual es la sopa de hoy?*"

"Today we have *sopa de gallina india y pan con chompipe.*"

"*¿Como suena,* Chele?"

"*Chompipe,* that's a new word. *No lo he probado,* but I'm sure it will be great." She did know about the Indian hens, black feathered with dark meat and very tasty. Not at all like boring American chicken.

"That's good because that's all they have. Lili cooks a different Salvadoran specialty every day, *pero solo una, verdad, Lili?*"

"*Si, hombre,* how much can one person do?"

"This is true. Since you do everything, there's no way you could have a bigger selection."

Manuel brings the food to the table that Shelly has chosen. Once they begin eating, Manuel tells Shelly, "I have something I need to tell you. It's the reason why Victor didn't give you my address and phone number. He would be very angry with me if he knew I told you, so you must—"

"*No se preocupe,* Manuel. It's highly unlikely I will ever see Victor again. When I leave here, I am flying back to New York, back to my family. I have come to see how important family is since I've been here."

"Well, that's what this is about ... family. You notice that Letty said she didn't know I had a brother? Well, the thing is I've always told people that Victor is my uncle."

"Manuel, why would you tell people that?"

"Because he *is* my uncle."

"So, you and Victor were lying? Victor lied to me?"

"No, he didn't lie, Chele. He is my uncle ... and he is my brother."

"But, Manuel, that doesn't make sense. That can't be––" Suddenly, Shelly looks at Manuel with a frown. Her eyebrows are scrunched together.

"My mother is Victor's sister so he is my uncle ... but my father is Victor's father so he is also my brother."

"Manuel ... I'm so-o ... sorry."

"The funny thing is, for Victor, that's it. That's his only complication. But he runs away from it. Me? What am I? My father's grandson? My mother's brother? Every familial relationship has a polar opposite for me, but do I run away?"

"Manuel, I'm not trying to be mean, but you *did* go to the US, and wouldn't you have stayed there if you could have continued your studies?"

"Chele, I can't say for sure, but I was relieved when I found out that none of my training counted there. It meant I could go home. And it meant that I could stop feeling guilty for who or what I am. Victor thinks that our family is cursed. And it's all because of me."

"He doesn't blame your ... his father? In the US, they would have put him in jail."

"My grandmother was concerned about my soul ... so she took me to church several times a week. Some of the priests know, because she told them in confession. Her main concern has always been that I should not have to pay for the sins of my father ... and my mother."

"Your mother? How old was she? Is she as strong as your ... her father? It is not her fault, no matter how things happened." Shelly's hands are flailing around in the air. "Why didn't her mother protect her? Where was your grandmother when this was happening?" She is speaking so loudly that Manuel has to shush her.

"That is why she took me to church," he says, almost in a whisper. "That is why she has been a second mother to me. To this day, some people think she is my mother. It is because of her I am becoming a doctor. And if I become a priest, it will also be because of her. She did not know what my father was doing to her daughter. So she also blames herself."

Ita Lili brings the food, so they sit quietly eating for some time.

Finally Shelly whispers, "Manuel, I promise to never tell anyone what you have told me. Not even Letty. You tell Letty whatever you want, but she will never hear about any of this from me."

"Thank you, Chele. Thank you ... for listening. I feel as if I have just confessed my sins. I don't know why I felt compelled to tell you. Maybe it is because you will leave and take the secret with you. But maybe it is the first step in accepting who I am. I don't know."

"There seems to be a lot of that going on around here."

Manuel looks at her quizzically, but Shelly says nothing more.

Chapter 27

Too many secrets, too many lies

After Manuel's confession, Shelly is feeling strange, kind of light-headed. She grabs hold of the chair to steady herself. *Why is everyone compelled to tell me their secrets? What makes them so sure I will not repeat them?* Now Shelly understands Victor's desolate brooding with everyone. With Shelly, he was different. She had met Manuel. No one else in the small group in New Orleans had. They called themselves brothers and in the US, that's all they had to be. No one there knew his family, so he could be Manuel's big brother and Shelly could be complicit in his secret. *Except ... I wasn't. I had no idea. And Victor never tried to tell me.*

Suddenly, Shelly wants to be home. *If not home back in New York, at least back at the Gonzalez home.* There are too many secrets, too many lies for one person to hold. But Shelly told Manuel she would go to the hospital, so they head in that direction. Manuel is such a gentleman; he keeps Shelly on the inside of the sidewalk and makes sure her pack is all zipped up. He even offers to carry it for her, which of course she refuses.

Manuel opens the door to *Hospital Bloom* and then guides Shelly to the area where he spends most of his time. "This is where the children with incurable diseases stay," he tells her.

As she walks around, looking at these ailing, half-dead children in this decrepit, unhygienic giant room, Manuel explains to her, "The parents had to leave the children here at the hospital. They had to go back to the countryside, back to their labor, which for most is working the land, someone else's land."

"Manuel, some of them are babies!" Shelly cries.

"The parents don't have any money and could not survive without working every day. They are barely surviving as it is."

"But, how do they pay for their child to be in the hospital?" She only asks because she can't stand to hear this sad story of these children any longer.

"Oh, I didn't tell you about Benjamin Bloom. He was an American who built the hospital so Salvadoran children would have access to health care. Maybe another American will help to bring attention to these children so they will not lie here alone until they die." Manuel smiles at her, but Shelly does not smile back. *How much can one person do?*

"The children are so sick they barely have the energy to eat ... and so depressed that the only way to get any response at all is to go over and look them in the eyes and talk to them," Manuel tells her, so that is what Shelly does.

"*¿Cómo te llamas, hijo? ¿De dónde eres?*"

The child looks at her, but can't seem to talk. Not enough energy to open his mouth, but he does manage to smile even though he winces afterward.

"Manuel, if I had known you were going to bring me here, I would have brought toys or candy or something."

"Yes, well, maybe next time. No candy, though. They are too sick to be eating candy."

As they leave, Shelly waves goodbye to all the children. She tells them, *"Les voy a ver muy pronto.* I love you, *preciosos."* Tears are welling up in Shelly's eyes, but she cannot let these children see her cry. *It won't make them feel any better. It would probably make them feel worse.*

Shelly contains her grief until they are in the elevator and then a torrent of tears begins to flow from her eyes and she is hyperventilating, trying to catch her breath. Manuel watches, unable to console her. If he allows himself to sympathize with her, he too will soon be crying uncontrollably. And then, who would take care of these children, forsaken by the world? So he lets her cry and they walk for half an hour in the streets, people staring, wondering what this young man has done to this woman to make her cry so inconsolably.

Chapter 28

Family

Abuela had told Shelly before going to bed she would be going in late to the Refugee Center. Shelly wishes she could let Ceci know in advance when she will be late, but the Gonzalez family never seems to think that far ahead. Luckily, Ceci is always happy to see her no matter when she shows up.

"We are meeting Paula at the hospital," Abuela says, "so don't forget your camera, Chele."

Shelly smiles. "Thank you for the breakfast, Abuela. And thank you for not minding my intrusive camera."

"Oh, I am used to it by now. And who knows? Maybe someday you will bring us a photo album with all these beautiful photos in them."

"Si, Abuela, quien sabe."

This hospital is very different from the one Manuel took her to. "Abuela, is this where the rich come when they are sick?"

"Si, mi amor. The rich get sick too, you know."

"Yeah, but who wouldn't mind being sick if you are going to be treated like a king!"

"Shhh, Chele. Someone will hear you. Besides, no one wants to have a sick loved one, whether you are rich or poor."

"Tiene razón, Abuela. I'm sorry."

"Don't worry about it, *amor*. I know you didn't mean anything by it. I could see you had been crying yesterday when you came home from seeing the children with Manuel."

"Abuela, do you know Manuel?"

"Well, I know about him. I know that he loves my granddaughter."

"Who told you? Letty?"

"No one, I could see it in the way he looks at her."

"You saw them together?"

"Now don't go making a fuss. I was out and happened to see them together."

"You happened to see them, huh? So that is what you used to do before I came? Spy on your family?"

"They won't tell me anything, so what else can I do? How am I going to find out what they are up to? How can I take care of them if I don't know why they are happy? Or sad?"

They walk past the guards, and Shelly says, "Abuela, why do they look like soldiers?"

"Shhh, they *are* soldiers, *mi amor*. This is their other job." They stop at the elevators and Abuela pushes the button for the fourth floor.

"How do you know which floor he is on?"

"Geriatrics is on the fourth floor."

"Geri-what?" Shelly asks.

"It is the study of old people's health, mi amor. You should try to learn a bit. We all get old eventually."

Shelly is still thinking about how Letty said her grandmother didn't know anything. *This woman is one of the wisest people I have ever met*, Shelly thinks. *After my own grandmother, of course.*

120

Abuela asks one of the nurses where Don Fernando's room is. She tells her, and then says, "Only family is allowed."

"Of course! This is his great-granddaughter from America."

"*Perdón, señora.* I didn't realize he had family in the US."

"No problem. How could you know?"

They walk down the clean white hallway. "Abuela, how can you lie like that?" Shelly whispers.

"Chele, someday you will learn. We do what we have to do in this life." Abuela gives Shelly a smile, but then frowns as she sees Paula outside the room. She gives her a big hug. Shelly notices that she is not at all uncomfortable being hugged by her friend. "Paula, is everything alright?"

"Shhh, Don Fernando's sons are in there. They are asking all kinds of questions."

"*Qué tipo de preguntas, Paula?*"

"They want to know about his will. When did he last update it? Where is it?"

"That is terrible, Paula. They should be trying to cheer *el Viejo* up. Not depressing him with questions like he could die any minute."

"Maeli, he *is* dying. He could go anytime now."

"Well, still, you don't browbeat a man on his deathbed!"

"Hush, they are coming out now." Paula turns and gives a little bow to the two men—men who look much older than Señor Gonzalez. "*Hijos,* I'm so sorr—"

"Don't call us that! We are not your sons. And don't think you are getting anything of his either. You have done everything but suck his blood out of him."

"Excuse me—!" Shelly shouts.

"Chele, don't get involved in this," Abuela tries to soothe her. She moves her over to a corner where they won't be heard.

"But, Abuela, they are so cruel!"

"I know, Chele, but Paula always knew they would be like this. They think she went after their father, knowing he was vulnerable because his wife was dying."

"Well, they obviously don't know anything!"

"Paula brought those boys up. That is the worst thing. But I suspect it is the older one. The younger son loved Paula like a mother. *Su madre* was already very sick by then, and Paula did everything. She even tried to suckle him, but she was just a child herself. "

Chapter 29

Adiós

After the men leave, Shelly takes a walk down to the cafeteria so Abuela can calm Paula down. Shelly is amazed at this hospital. It is fancier than any she's been to; even the Catholic hospital in Rochester wasn't this nice and that was not only in the US, but it was also where the rich went.

Shelly finds Abuela and Paula in the room with Don Fernando. She has her camera, but she wasn't expecting to feel this emotional. Paula has stopped crying and when she sees Shelly, she hugs her this time. Shelly wonders what Abuela has told her that would make her feel so comfortable now.

"Don Fernando is dying," Abuela tells her.

"I am so sorry, Paula. You must have loved him very much."

"He was all I had after my parents were killed. *Y sus hijos*, of course, but you saw how they feel about me."

"They are hurting, Paula. And like my mother always says, 'You always hurt the ones you love.' Someday, they will realize all that you did for them."

"Oh, *Maeli*, I hope so."

"Paula has a favor to ask you. She has no pictures of her and Don Fernando together. And she doubts she

123

will be given any photos of Don Fernando."

"So, Chele, I was hoping you would take a few pictures of us."

Shelly can't say no to this woman, so she pulls out her camera and starts shooting. "Paula, move in close so I can get a close-up of your faces." Paula does everything Shelly asks. Shelly remembers the time she helped a gentleman do a wedding. She hadn't wanted to, but he had been persistent. Now she realizes she had learned something from him, so she tells Paula to put her hand next to Don Fernando's, then to hold his hand.

Don Fernando opens his eyes and moans, "*¿Paulita, dónde está, mi niña?*"

"*Aquí estoy, Don jefe. Qué quiere, mi amor.*" Shelly looks at Abuela and the older woman shakes her head.

"Paulita, I have to tell you something. It is about *tus padres*," Don Fernando tells her. Abuela gets up, her eyes darting nervously around the room.

"*Don Jefe*, let's not talk about that. Let's talk about the good times."

"Paulita, this is important. I need you ... to ... know. It is terrible what I did."

"No, Don Fernando, it is not terrible. You let me stay on when I had nowhere to go."

"But, it is my fault. I did it, Paula, and I know it was wrong." Don Fernando is getting agitated and Abuela looks like she has seen a ghost. She stumbles out and tells a nurse to come in. "Paula, *por favor, escúchame. Esto es ... muy ... importante.*" Don Fernando can barely breathe, let alone talk.

The nurse rushes in. "Calm down, Don Fernando.

You must calm down."

"Pero tengo algo que decir ... a ... mi ... Paulita."

"I'm sorry, but you are all going to have to leave now."

"But, nurse, he has a confession to make. Why won't you let him?"

"That confession could kill him, señorita! Besides, you should bring a priest in to hear his confession. And give him last rites too."

So they all say *"Adiós"* to Don Fernando. As they walk out, Paula thanks Shelly five or six times. Shelly tries never to make a promise about the photos to any of the subjects, but this time she tells Paula that she will send copies of these photos to Abuela so she can have them.

After Paula leaves and Shelly and Abuela are out of the hospital, she shouts, "Abuela, why didn't you let him tell her? She has a right to know what this man did to her parents."

"No, Chele, some things are better left unsaid. Do you think Paula is going to feel any better knowing this about the father of her child?"

"We all deserve to know the truth, no matter how much it hurts."

"How many more lives need to be ruined? It has already been so many. Let Paula have her memories."

"But they are false memories. They are all lies!"

"No, Chele, the memories are real. And Don Fernando felt remorse for what he did."

"How do you know?"

"Because he was dying. He could have taken the knowledge with him. But he wanted Paula to know because he felt terrible about what he did."

"*Ayyy*, Abuela, I don't understand."

"You will, *hija*. You will. Someday. Let God decide his punishment. Let God decide if Paula ever needs to know that the man she loved like a father and a husband killed her parents. Only God can make these kinds of decisions."

"I hope you are right, Abuela. I hope someday I will understand."

Chapter 30

Suspicion

At the center, Shelly goes through the motions. As always, she can hear Ceci taking down the stories of how these women came to be refugees. Today though, she really hears what these women are saying.

This woman had her little home torn apart as the soldiers looked for *subversivos*, young men who were going against the government. They found her husband and when they realized he was trying to stop them from looking in the trunk, they shot him. Then they opened the trunk and found their teenage son. The woman is sobbing as she answers Ceci's question, "What did they do with the boy?"

"They took him with them. They said they would make a soldier out of him. But I don't want my son to be a soldier, not if he is going to learn to be like them!" she cries.

It occurs to Shelly that she has been doing the same thing the refugee women do, going into her own head and thinking about other times, remembering better times, rather than hearing what these women are saying. As she continues photographing the women, she hears the next story.

"They pulled my husband out of the *casita*. They pull out their machete. My husband looks at me, trying to tell me with his eyes not to look, but like a fool, I do look. They lay his head on one of the pieces of tree trunk that my Jose had cut for us, one for each family member to sit on after the sun goes down and it cools off a bit. They put his head there ... and they chop it off."

Shelly notices that Ceci is quiet. Normally she would be asking for more details, but this time she can't bring herself to speak.

The woman continues. "The soldiers are laughing ... and I am screaming, except that nothing is coming out of my mouth. They grab a stick and pound it into the ground right in front of our little home, where everyone in town can see, and they grab Jose's head by his hair and place it on top of the stick. By that time, I am vomiting all over the house, but I know I must grab my children and keep them quiet." She begins to cry, and both Shelly and Ceci breathe a sigh of relief. At least she still has her children. But when Shelly looks over, she realizes that this is one of the women Shelly brought the street children to meet. She does not have her children with her. *Where are they?* Shelly wonders.

"*¡Ven a jugar!*" Shelly hears the shouts of children calling after Miguelito to come play with them.

"No," he tells them, "I have work to do." The street vendors call to him too. He waves and keeps on running into the center. He asks Ceci where Señor John is.

"He's gone. He'll be back next week," she says. "What's wrong, Miguel?"

Shelly notices that Ceci is the only one who calls this boy Miguel, not Miguelito.

"¿Y la señorita Chele? ¿Dónde esta ella?"

"Aqui estoy, Miguelito. ¿Qué te pasa?" Shelly responds.

Miguelito won't speak. Or can't speak. Shelly is not sure which. He pulls her arm. Finally he manages to say, *"Agarre su camera.* Come with me."

As Miguelito pulls her past the street vendor and the children, Shelly waves to them, but she is already preparing herself for something she does not want to see. She knows, by Miguelito's demeanor, that this is going to keep her up at night.

When they arrive, a small crowd has gathered. The police and military strut around. Some local priests and nuns are clustered in a circle. There is a woman taking photos and two men are standing in a hole in the earth. Everyone is staring at the three bodies lying on the ground, covered with dirt. The dead women's milky white skin is muddied, bruised, and broken. These women are not Salvadoran. Though she is shaking, Shelly takes the camera dangling from her neck. *I know I should do this. I said I would do this.*

A colonel struts over and asks who she is. "Show me your ID." She pulls her passport out of her chest purse bought for this purpose. "No, I need to see your press ID. *¿Qué está haciendo aquí?"*

She doesn't know what to tell him. *What am I doing here?*

Miguelito suddenly says, *"Ella es mi ti*a, my aunt from the US. *Solo está de visita."*

"Then why do you want to take pictures of this? If you are only visiting?" He is looking at her suspiciously.

One of the men who unearthed the bodies comes over and starts talking to the colonel. The woman taking photographs catches Shelly's eye. It is amazing what one can say without saying a word. *I completely understood that she would take the photos, that I should not put my life in danger.*

"Who are they?" Shelly whispers to one of the nuns.

At that same instant, she hears the colonel shouting to the Salvadoran journalists, "They were Americans, guerrillas, pretending to be nuns."

The nun answers me. "*Las monjas americanas.* They've been here for several years helping the poor. We were all afraid this would happen."

It occurs to Shelly that no one is safe here. *It doesn't matter who you are or where you're from. If they don't like what you're doing, you could be killed.*

"They knew they could be killed. They said God would take them when he was ready," she continues. Shelly knows now that she must decide if she is willing to give her life for these people. *Or do I run home to my safe little life and try to forget what is happening here?*

"¡*Mártires!¡ Son mártires para la revolucion!*" Shelly hears a young man's voice, though she has no idea where it is coming from. *A martyr for the revolution, is that what I want to be?*

Chapter 31

Beyond comprehension

Shelly wakes early before the sun comes up, and though she can't leave the house until it is light out, she wants to be out the door as soon as she sees the sun peek out from the mountaintops.

It's 4:30 a.m. and Abuela already has a big breakfast ready: eggs, beans, tortillas, and orange juice. Shelly tells her, "I don't know how late I will be today. I have something I need to do."

"I will pack you a lunch, Chele. Promise me that you will be careful."

"*No se preocupe*, Abuela, I'm always careful." Again Shelly wonders how she knows that today is different from any other day. Shelly grabs a jacket, though she doubts she'll need it, and puts on her tennis shoes. She has been told she should wear a skirt to the prison, but she puts shorts on underneath it. At least when she gets frisked there will be an extra layer between her and the guard's hands. She puts a T-shirt on under her blouse too.

Abuela puts delicious black bean and *queso con loroco* sandwiches in Shelly's backpack. Shelly gets excited about the prospect of eating this Salvadoran delicacy, then realizes that if she can get into the prison, she will be leaving them there for Mayra.

Shelly walks to the bus stop, saying hello to neighbors as she passes them. A soccer ball rolls into the street. It's the one Shelly brought from the US. The kids smile and ask her to play with them. "*La próxima vez*," she tells them. They laugh and repeat it. That's what she always tells them, but *next time* never seems to come.

Shelly stands with several older women waiting for the bus. She can smell the hot tortillas one woman is carrying. Judging from the mixture of aromas another woman must have *pupusas*. There's no place to sit because the cement bench has been blown apart, whether by the army or the guerrillas she does not know. *I guess the effect is the same either way: no place for a woman weary from hard work and the war to sit and rest her bones.*

The bus can be heard from a few blocks away, but the children run up to tell her, "*¡Ita Chele, hay viene el camión!*"

"*Gracias, mis niños lindos, gracias.*" Shelly feels a twist in her heart. *These kids are so sweet. I just know when I leave, it will be hardest to leave them behind.*

Shelly steps onto the rumbling, shaking bus and tells the driver, "*Voy a la Prisión de mujeres.*" She looks up at the pictures of the Virgin Mary next to photos of naked women plastered all over above the windshield. *I'll never understand how these men can justify looking at the Madonna and women that make you think about sex at the same time. It is beyond my comprehension.*

"*Si, señorita, alli vamos,*" he answers back. The other women don't say anything. They just pay their fare.

Shelly is walking, more like stumbling, intent on getting to the back of the bus. A middle-aged man, dressed in dirty old clothes gets up and insists she take his seat. She tells him, *"Nó, estoy bien,"* but he refuses to accept no for an answer. She looks at his face and knows that it will make him feel better if she sits and he stands, despite the fact that he could use the rest. So she takes off her backpack and sits down. He smiles at her before he heads to the back of the bus.

Shelly turns to look at the others on the bus and can't help but notice how brown and calloused all the men's hands are. It's the first time Shelly realizes how much hard work, *really* hard work, ages people. Most of the men are bent at the waist, no longer able to stand up straight, and though they look fifty or sixty, they are probably much younger than that. Shelly remembers reading that the average life expectancy for a man in El Salvador is about thirty-seven years old. By their standard, she supposes they *are* old.

Everyone is quiet getting off the bus, but as soon as they are all off, several people, mostly women, begin shouting. *"¡Tortillas!"* yells one.

"¡Pupusas!" yells another. They are selling food to the people going to the prison. They also have buns filled with black beans and cheese, like the ones Abuela made for Shelly, and sodas.

Shelly looks at the sodas, but the woman says, "They cannot be taken into the prison." *I guess I am the only new visitor today. Everyone else seems to know exactly what they can and can't do.*

Shelly waits for everyone to finish buying their items, as she doesn't want to go alone. They quietly finish their business and Shelly follows them.

At the prison, they tell them, *"Hagan una linea*

para la Prision de mujeres. Make another line if you are going to the men's prison." Again Shelly gets to the back of the line. She watches them frisk the women and is thankful for the extra layer of padding she's added. She notices the other women have done the same. Shelly dreaded this more than anything, but they are quick with her. *Probably because I'm American. Or maybe they just want to finish up and take a break.*

Shelly notices they take one woman away to interrogate her more, and her heart begins to pound. Carlos had told her to stay calm. He said that they look for signs of nervousness: sweating, stuttering, and other such indications.

Remembering his words of advice only makes Shelly more nervous, so she pushes it out of her mind and begins to recite the prayers Abuela taught her, *God grant me the serenity to accept the things I cannot change, the courage to change...*

"*¿A quién vá a ver, señorita?*" the lieutenant asks her. It occurs to Shelly that they should not see her praying, either. *That might be another sign I'm guilty of something, God knows what.*

"*A Mayra Rodriguez Silva,*" she answers.

"*¿Y cuál es su relación?*" She doesn't answer. She doesn't know what to say. "What is she to you, miss?" He frowns at her, not liking her hesitation.

"*Familia, del lado de mi mamá,*" she finally blurts out. *It is the one thing they respect here, family relationships.* The lieutenant relaxes his shoulders and Shelly knows she is in the clear. At least for now.

"You will have fifteen minutes from the time you enter the cell--if you can stand it that long." He laughs and so do the other guards. Shelly cannot believe these visitors take a whole day off, when they are barely surviving, to spend fifteen minutes with their loved ones.

Her heart is pounding again as she follows the guard down a hallway, then down two flights of cement stairs. The closer they get to the cells, the more sobbing, moaning, and screaming Shelly hears. The smell of urine and feces gets stronger too. Shelly is feeling faint when the guard finally opens the cell door to Mayra. She looks at her thin, gaunt body and gasps. Shelly turns back toward the cell door and yells, "Guard, there must be some mistake! I am here to see Mayra Rodriguez Silva!"

"*Soy yó*," she says, whispering hoarsely.

"But they said you were twenty-nine years old!"

"That is correct. I turn thirty next month," she answers slowly. Just speaking seems to take all her energy.

She looks closer to eighty years old. She can't weigh much more than eighty pounds, maybe seventy-five. And her eyes are sunk deep into her skull. Her skin is wrinkled and hangs on her body like a piece of clothing. But her hair is still black, which is the only reason Shelly is prepared to believe that she might actually be twenty-nine.

She is sitting on a bucket, probably where she would usually go to the bathroom. There is a cement table in front of her, which Shelly realizes, as she looks around, has to be her bed too. And in front of that is a round cement stool that looks like it had been made in a pail similar to the one she is sitting on. "Forgive me for not getting up. I spent all my energy preparing for your visit. Please sit down."

"You knew I was coming? But how is that possible?"

"Mis compañeros no me han abandonado – despite the fact that I wasn't with them before I was arrested and thrown in jail. Since we're only allowed one visitor a week, they came to see another *compañera* and yelled to me from her cell that you were coming."

"But I hadn't even decided until yesterday to come, and I told no one ... You said you weren't with them when you were arrested?" Shelly decides not to waste her precious time trying to figure out how everyone else seems to know her every move even before she does. She will figure that out later. Perhaps.

"No, I was a journalist. A good journalist doesn't take sides. But I began reporting about the massacres and investigating the killings of the priests. They weren't printing anything, so I guess the owner of the newspaper must have reported me to the police. I knew I was being followed, but I continued to do my work the way I was trained to do."

"So what happened?" Shelly asks, still trying to connect this Mayra to the Mayra she is telling her about. She can't imagine this frail woman being such a headstrong journalist, especially in a country where women in any position of power are almost nonexistent.

"Probably my downfall was wanting to interview and write about the *frente*. It is not that hard to get in touch with the guerrillas. You just have to mention it to someone and it won't be long before they get back to you. I had made my contacts and was getting ready to go. I was waiting for the photographer, so when I heard a knock at the door, I just assumed it was him. Instead the police broke down the door before I could get to it to open it, which I would have done. I had nothing to hide."

"So you never even made it to meet with them?" Shelly is turning red with anger, but also feels a profound sadness for this woman. Yet she is shaking with fear too. *Someone had to have reported her, someone she trusted. How does one trust anyone here?*

"No, I was brought here that day. They have beaten me, raped me, and used the electrical prod on me, but I can't tell them anything because I don't know anything."

"What do they want to know?" Shelly is crying despite her promises not to. *How can this happen to someone who is just doing her job?*

"They want names. They want to arrest more people. They want to torture more people. They don't even care who they are, or if they're innocent. Some of the prisoners give names just to stop the torture, but it doesn't stop. Chances are, if they think you've told them everything you know they'll kill you anyway. So what's the use? Why get more people hurt when it's not going to even help you?"

"*¡Dos minutos más!*" the guard yells.

"Mayra, I think you know … that they want me to photograph you. I just don't know … if I could risk my life like that," Shelly whispers, barely able to speak.

"It's okay. You do what you can. We all do what we can. Don't let anyone pressure you to do anything you don't want to do. This is your life and no one else can live it for you."

Shelly hugs her as tears run down her face and all over her blouse. She sets down the black bean sandwiches and turns to walk away. Then she realizes: *this is why I brought my jacket today.* She pulls it out of her backpack and lays it down on the concrete slab. Mayra picks it up and lovingly caresses and smells it. She manages to smile. "Thank you," she says, tears now rolling down her cheeks too, "I will never forget the *norteamericana* who came halfway across the world for me."

Shelly wipes her face with her skirt as the guard opens the door. She follows him quietly back up the stairs. As she listens to the moans and cries, she hears someone say, "Tell Carlos thank you for us."

As soon as Shelly gets outside, she runs over to some bushes. Her entire breakfast comes out onto the ground: eggs, beans, tortillas, and orange juice. She turns around and one of the women vendors hands her a bottle of water and a rag, probably a piece of a worn-out dress. As the woman turns around, Shelly says, *"Señora, su dinero."*

"¿No te preocupas, niña. Cuidáte, oís?" She pushes the money back at Shelly. *I wish I didn't have to worry about anything, but yes, I will take care of myself ... to the best of my ability.*

Chapter 32

Cooking smells

Ceci smiles and watches Shelly watering the plants. She can't believe that Shelly actually has them growing, that there are flowers blooming all over the courtyard.

Shelly looks at her and smiles back. "What is the song you were humming?" Ceci asks.

"Oh, I don't know. Just something my grandmother used to have my mom play on the stereo." *I no longer have trouble saying "grandmother." After all, the woman did everything a grandmother would do, so what difference does it make?*

"John's back for a couple days." Shelly looks at the door of the Refugee Center. John stands there waiting, looking more like a soldier protecting his citizens than a photographer. "He wants to take us to lunch."

"Ceci, that is sweet of you, but you probably want to spend the time alone with him."

Ceci winks at Shelly and says, "We'll have time for that later. John insists that buying you lunch is the least he could do to compensate for you taking care of the work here."

"*Señoras,*" Ceci shouts, "we'll be back in *pues, una hora, más o menos.*"

Shelly notices the women smile and answer back, "*Qué les vaya bien. Hasta pronto.*" She smiles at them and breathes a sigh of relief. The three of them wave as they walk out the door.

As they sit in the restaurant, Shelly looks around at bright blues, pinks and reds. A *quetzal* is painted on one wall. A mountain with a lake in front of it on another. The room is filled with smells: beans, tortillas, seafood, every kind of pork dish imaginable.

"So, Shelly, how are you doing? Getting to know the country?"

Shelly stares at John, not knowing what to say. *Sure, I am getting to know the fucked up legal system, if you want to call it that. No trial; no "get out of jail free" cards. Go straight to prison and torture.*

"Sorry, I guess that was my attempt at humor. Of course, there are some beautiful things to see here. Beaches and fancy restaurants. Some very elegant hotels––if you have the money."

"Yeah, I know. And taxis for the rich and the foreigners. I already got the lecture about the dangers of taking the bus."

"Don't worry about it. Salvadorans are very protective of us foreigners. They are used to putting themselves in danger, but they would feel terrible if anything happened to one of us."

The waitress comes over and John orders three specials. Shelly doesn't bother to say she's a vegetarian. She just hopes the rice and beans don't have too much lard in them. Her stomach will not stand another day like she had yesterday.

She watches John and Ceci holding hands, whispering and laughing. "Sorry, Shelly. It's been ten days since we last saw each other."

"Don't worry about me. I'm fine."

"Chele is a quiet soul," Ceci tells him. "She only talks when it is necessary, right?" Ceci winks at Shelly.

"Yeah, I learned that from my dad. My mom hates that he is like that."

"How are things going with the Agrarian Reform?" Shelly manages to ask.

"Sorry, but we don't talk about that stuff in public," John whispers. "Those words are curse words to the powers that be. Let's see ... what *can* we talk about? Well, Shelly, how do you like this family you are living with? Are they treating you well?"

"Oh, the Gonzalezes are great. They treat me like I am a part of their family."

"If you stay here long enough, you will learn that the poor and the not-so-poor are all like that. I never have to worry about a place to stay when we cover the news in the countryside. Several families always offer to take me in. Then I have to hide money under the sugar bowl because they won't take a cent for letting me stay the night and eat their food."

The waitress fills the table with the three specials; thick tortillas, black beans, rice, *curtido,* and chicken. Shelly breathes a sigh of relief. *The chicken doesn't upset my stomach if I don't eat too much.* "Well, it looks like some hungry child is going to get fed today," Shelly says with a laugh, knowing they totally agree with giving their leftovers to one of the boys hanging around looking for a handout.

They all eat quietly as Shelly watches the couple speak volumes with their eyes. Their smiles seem to permeate the place and the colors look even brighter. *I've never seen two people more in love.*

Chapter 33

No one must know

Back at the center, Shelly finishes out the day. Feeling like she needs a break from the sadness, she decides to take a different route back to the Gonzalez home. As long as she keeps track of her left and right turns, she can find her way home. Besides, she can always look for a taxi if she gets lost.

As she turns a corner, Shelly sees Isabel hugging a man. She steps back behind a building and watches them. They look concerned, agitated, yet they comfort each other. The man goes in one direction and Isabel walks toward Shelly so she steps out from the side of the building and pretends to be surprised. "Isabel, what are you doing here?"

"Chele, is this the way you go home? It is a strange way."

"No, not usually. Isabel, is everything alright?"

"No, Chele. Not at all." Shelly looks at her, surprised. "Come, let's get a coffee. This way. I know a place a couple blocks up."

Once inside the quaint little café, Isabel orders for them both, "A pot of *café con leche*, sweetened with honey. Let's sit in the corner so we can see the door."

"Okay, but please tell me who that man was I saw you hugging."

"That was Samuel."

Shelly is stumped for words. *Juan Jr.'s father. His real father.*

"Isabel, does he know about Juan Jr.?"

"*Si ... y no.* He knows I have a son, but no, he does not know that he is the father of my son. We were out of contact for several years, but then a few years ago, when I was visiting my grandparents, I decided to go say hello. I wanted to see the family my mother pretends doesn't exist."

"But Isabel, you know it was not her decision, right?"

"That was what I wanted to find out. Listen, Chele, no one must know about this."

Shelly lets out a long sigh. *So, what else is new?*

"My father's been arrested."

"Oh, no, Isabel, why? What did he do?" *Stupid question, Shelly.*

"Alberto, my father, is a teacher, but he began organizing teachers years ago, getting them involved in the teacher's union." Shelly can't help but think of the irony: *Her father who she never knew and her husband are both union organizers.* "He has been arrested before, but they released him after a couple days. Samuel doesn't think they will release him this time. They no longer care who somebody is, or if their family has money."

It occurs to Shelly that if Isabel's father isn't safe, neither is her husband.

"But what can you do?"

"Probably nothing, but Samuel wanted me to know."

Shelly just stares at Isabel, noticing how much older she looks in the few months since she first met her.

They sit quietly for some time, looking at their

coffee. Neither feels like drinking it. Shelly has many questions, but she is not used to asking. This family has always answered her unasked questions.

"Is there anything I can do?"

"Si, Chele. I will tell Juan I am taking you to see my grandparents so you can photograph them. Since they are in their late eighties, he can't deny us that."

"Okay, I will go." Although Shelly has been wanting to go to Sonsonante, she thinks, *Not like this*.

"Samuel is very concerned about his grandparents, *my grandparents*. They are so old, this could kill them."

"Oh, Isabel, I am so sorry." And she truly is sorry. *Old people should be able to leave this world in peace like my grandmother did.*

Chapter 34

An enigma

Shelly puts her camera on the upper shelf and takes the window seat on the air-conditioned bus. Isabel sits in the aisle seat. She has one bag with a change of clothes and her wallet. Shelly watches as everyone else finds seats. "This looks like a tourist bus. I've never taken one but I have seen them before."

"Yes, Chele, this is a tourist bus. Not many of us have cars. Besides, taking a car into the countryside is not a good idea."

Shelly doesn't bother to ask why. Between soldiers, guerrillas, and bandits taking advantage of the situation, one would likely lose their car and be lucky if they didn't lose their life.

"I guess some people have money in this country."

"Yes, Chele, of course. You have to have the rich, or nothing would happen. No homes being built. No businesses started, to hire workers. Nothing."

"Hmmm, I never thought of that."

"There are many things we don't think about. We also need progressive thinkers and professionals: doctors, engineers. So, these people have a little money and they have to have a way to get back to see their families, just like you and I are doing."

Shelly stays quiet for some time, watching the changes in the environment, seeing shantytowns, then decent houses, then shantytowns again. She remembers what Letty said, that it won't always be like this. "Do you think some rich people might decide to invest in this country again so more people can have a better life?"

"I don't know, Chele, but I pray that someday people will have homes and be able to go to school. I pray that all this mess, this fighting," Isabel whispers, "I pray morning and night that it will lead to something good, but who knows?"

The bus has stopped again. It is countryside; no houses can be seen. Some young men and one woman get on. The bus driver sits calmly and lights a cigarette like it is break time. Some of the young men have on fatigues, but Shelly can tell they aren't soldiers. One has on a T-shirt that has Pepsi Cola on it. They are all wearing some kind of hat—a baseball cap on one, a beret on another's head, a straw hat on the woman's. They wear the hats down low enough to partially cover their faces.

The young woman has on jeans and a long-sleeved shirt, the sleeves rolled up above her elbows. The others walk behind her. They all have different kinds of guns, but do not point them at anyone. She takes her hat off and holds it in front of her. *"Ayuda a la causa Salvadoreña, la causa de los campesinos, por favor,"* she says. Shelly thinks of Ana and wonders if these guerrillas know her. *Maybe they even know Carlos*, she thinks.

Everyone puts *something* in—some throw in some change, others a *colón* or two. When they get to Shelly's row, Isabel throws in twenty *colones* and says,

"*Para nosotros dos.*" Shelly looks at her, surprised. Is this the same woman who just told her they need the rich? *I don't know much more about Isabel now than the day I met her. She is such an enigma.*

The guerrillas finish quickly and get off the bus. One of them shouts, "*¡Viva la Revolución Salvadoreña!*" and they run into the trees as quickly as they arrived.

The bus driver puts out his cigarette and continues on his way.

It is dark by the time they arrive in Sonsonante. They walk quickly up the hill to a neighborhood where the homes need paint, but otherwise don't look so bad.

Isabel knocks softly and her grandmother opens the door. "*Shhh, tu abuelo ya esta dormido.* Your beds are made. *Nos vemos en la mañana.*"

Chapter 35

Delicious

The next morning, Isabel wakes Shelly up. "I don't know how long I'll be gone. Just spend time with my grandparents until I get back."

"You don't want me to go with you?"

"No, Chele, I am sorry, but I don't know what things will be like there, how my grandparents will be doing. I doubt they want to meet anyone right now."

"That's alright. I'll be okay here with Abuela's parents."

"Yes, you will love them both, I'm sure."

"What time is it?"

"Five a.m. I want to get there early. I know they aren't getting much sleep and it will make them feel better to see me."

"Alright. I am going back to sleep now." Shelly yawns and pulls the pillow over her head.

A Couple of Hours Later
Shelly gets dressed and then quietly tiptoes down the stairs, suddenly feeling shy in this strange house. She only met Abuela's mother for a second before they were rushed up to bed.

"There she is!" shouts Abuela's father.

Oh my God, I forgot to ask Isabel the names of her grandparents!

"Don't be shy. We know all about you, sweet angel. Coming all the way to our beloved country to try to help," says Abuela's mother.

"But I don't know what to call you both."

"Oh, this is my husband of sixty-some years."

"Ay, Antonia, she doesn't need our life story. I am Bernardo and this is my beautiful wife, Antonia."

"And we fixed every breakfast food we could think of, since Isabel said she was not sure what you were used to eating." The table is filled with pancakes, fruit, and yogurt. Then eggs and black beans and cheese. For drinks, there is coffee, orange juice, and milk. "If you prefer something else, we can see what we can do."

"Oh, no. That's so kind of you. Abuela and I usually just have *pan dulce*, the sweet bread from the local bakery."

"Oh, my, Maria Elizabeth was not brought up like that. We are so sorry."

"No, no, Maria ... Abuela offered to make me all these foods, but where I am from, we either eat cereal or skip breakfast altogether. I am not used to eating a big breakfast." Shelly feels her face getting hot. "Can I just take the photos and eat later?"

"You must eat something. How about a pancake and some coffee?" Reluctantly, Shelly sits down to eat, but does end up eating a pancake with some yogurt and fruit on top. Bernardo and Antonia talk away the entire time she is eating, telling her about their town and how they only had the one child. And how they never see their great-grandchildren, but Isabel visits every couple months.

"That was delicious! Thank you. Now can I photograph the two of you?"

Chapter 36

Discovery

Shelly looks around the house while Bernardo and Antonia change their clothes. She finds a little reading room with a wine-colored velvet loveseat, or what her grandmother called a settee. Since the room is rather dark, Shelly turns on the two lamps and then brings in a lamp from the living room to use as fill light. "Perfect," Shelly says out loud, though no one is there to hear her.

The couple walk down the steps wearing dress clothes from the thirties; *vintage* is what Shelly's generation calls them. "Oh, you both look stunning!" Shelly has a huge smile on her face as she takes Antonia's hand to help her down the stairs.

"This was our honeymoon outfit, though we didn't get to wear it for very long. Antonia must have become pregnant with Maria Elizabeth on the same night we were married. We had to come back home because she got terribly sick every time she ate."

"Bernardo, you were in as much of a hurry as I to get back home and start putting away our gifts and making the house a home."

Shelly is slowly guiding them to the little sitting room she found.

"Yes, *mi amor*, of course I wanted to get home, but I didn't expect things to happen so quickly!"

"Chelita, how did you know this was the right room? That settee was one of our wedding gifts. We come in here every night to read before we go to bed."

Shelly motions for them to sit down. "Since you are telling me about your first years of marriage, why don't you talk about that while I take the photos?"

"*Está bién, Chelita.* Mi Bernardito was the love of my life, but I had to hide my feelings. As you know, we women should never be the ones who show our love first. We must make the man feel he has won us over." Shelly remembers her grandmother giving her that same advice, though so far she has yet to use it.

"Antonia did not know that I loved her already. I was afraid she would reject me for someone more handsome or with more money."

"Ay, Bernardo, you always had those crazy ideas, like I was some silly schoolgirl who couldn't see what mattered most in a man." They laugh and look at each other and smile.

"Once we had Maria Elizabeth, we already had our daily rituals in place. Our parents fought over their granddaughter, each worrying the other would get more time with her."

"Had we known she would be our only child, we would have kept her all to ourselves. She was such a good girl, though; everyone wanted to help us with her. And when the church offered her a *beca* to go to the Catholic school, how could we say no?"

"Then before we knew it, she was grown and in love." Shelly shifts a little, all the while taking shots that she knows are going to be stunning.

"We knew Alberto. He was from a really good

family."

Shelly is tempted to ask what happened, but she has promised herself to let the truth come out on its own. She would never want anyone to feel bad or embarrassed because she asked too much.

"Oh, yes, of course, he was from a good family. His mother and I were in the same groups at church. She often brought *Albertito* with her when he cried and refused to stay with the nanny."

"Yes, he was a good boy and grew up to become a good man."

"Now, don't you go blaming me for what happened. You went along with everything I said."

"Yes, I know I did. And I will regret it for the rest of my life."

"Bernardo, stop that right now! We have discussed this so many times. Besides, it is too late now."

"I was the one with insomnia. I was the one who went to her bedroom door, night after night, listening to her cries. It's a miracle that baby turned out normal with all the crying she heard from her mother."

Shelly thinks of her own mother. *Did she cry because she didn't have a father?*

"Yes, you heard her cry, but I was the one making sure they both ate. I was the one trying to make my daughter see what a gift she had in her beautiful Isabel."

"I know, *Mami*, I know you were the best mother and grandmother anyone could have. Still though, I am sorry for what Maria Elizabeth had to go through. Never knowing that the man she loved, the father of her child, really did love her with all his heart."

Shelly stops taking photos now, hoping to hear what happened.

"Bernardito, you know it was the right thing. Alberto was already involved in the union. We both knew how determined he was."

"Yes, a very determined, hard-working, and good man. The kind of man any father would be proud to have as his son-in-law."

Shelly finally can't help herself. "I don't understand. If he was a good man and loved Abuela, why would he deny his child?"

"Oh, sweetheart, he never denied that Isabel was his."

"No, on the contrary, he came to me to ask if he could marry our daughter."

Shelly is staring at them both, her mouth agape. *Isn't love all you need to be happy?*

"Bernardo and I were expecting him and we had talked. As much as we loved Alberto, we could not ... it was a ... very difficult time ... in the country."

"There had been a bloodbath a few years earlier."

"A massacre. They killed union members."

"And jailed the leaders."

"But no one ever told Abuela?"

"That was Alberto's decision. He knew we were right. He knew he would be putting the woman he loved and his daughter in danger."

"He was such a gentleman. But, he said if he saw the love of his life ... and his child again, he could never leave them."

"So he quietly left for the capitol and never came back."

Shelly is stunned. *All these years, Abuela thought Alberto didn't love her. And it wasn't true.* She wants to make them tell Abuela the truth, but she knows it is not her place to be telling this old couple what to do. They were protecting the only daughter and grandchild they would ever have. Tears begin to fall down her cheeks, so Shelly excuses herself and runs to the bathroom to have a good cry.

As she sits on the bathtub, she realizes she loves Abuela as much as she loved her own grandmother. *It isn't fair. At least, my grandfather made his own choices. Abuela and Alberto did this because of this country, because of its terrible history.*

Chapter 37

A promise

Shelly knows already that John has only a couple more days in San Salvador, before he goes back to cover the Agrarian Reform. She must catch him now. When she gets to the center, she doesn't even notice that they painted the walls and there are more miniatures in new shadow boxes. She barely notices the women shouting hello to her.

John turns around and smiles. "Shelly, you're all caught up in your work, so take a day off if you like."

But Shelly isn't smiling back.

"Ceci, I need to talk to you and John. It is urgent. We need to talk privately."

After Shelly explains what she knows about Alberto's situation, Ceci and John say together, "The US embassy is our only chance to save him."

"Chele, you and John must go together. It is better if you are both Americans. And you can say he is a distant relative. You both must go *now*."

As Shelly and John walk to the embassy, they get their stories straight. John says, "Shelly, you need to stay quiet and let me speak. No matter what. Do you understand?"

"Yes, Okay. If that is what you think is best."

"Yes, that is best. You need to be tough."

"Okay. I promise to be stronger than I've ever been in my life."

When they arrive, John tells the guard, "We need to speak to the American ambassador. It is a matter of national security."

Once inside the building, one of the few made entirely out of marble, Shelly has to stuff her anger down once again. *Why did I not notice the huge gap between the rich and the poor before?* The embassy officials guide them into a large room with a huge wooden table surrounded by about twenty chairs. John and Shelly sit at one end and the ambassador, Mr. Alexander, at the other end.

"We are here to discuss a matter of grave importance. There is a teacher, Alberto Suarez Espinoza from Sonsonante, being held in prison here in San Salvador." John is using his most serious and professional voice.

"Well, what did he do to get put in prison?"

"He is a union organizer. That is why he is there."

"Sir and madam," the ambassador looks at them both, "there's no law against being a union organizer, so tell me, please, what else did this man do?"

Shelly's eyes are huge and she doesn't realize she is holding her breath. John had warned her not to speak unless specifically asked a question. He knows Shelly better than she knows herself. Shelly cannot help but get emotional, but logic is the key to getting Alberto released. The US embassy and even the government itself couldn't care less about emotions.

John clears his throat. "Sir, this man is a relative of Shelly Marie Smith. We are ready to contact as many as fifty unions as soon as we walk out this door if that is what it takes to get this man, this great educator and union leader, released from prison."

"I don't think that will be—"

"Sir, I am not finished," John's voice is loud and

deep. "We are ready to initiate protests in as many as fifty US cities, as well as cities in other countries throughout the world."

"Sir, we do not control the Salvadoran government. It is not up to us to decide their laws or who they put in prison, let alone who they take out of their prisons."

"Our government has given thirty million dollars to the Salvadoran government so far this year. Our government sent the weapons from Vietnam here. Our government that has set a limit of fifty US military advisors—"

"Okay, I get the picture. Leave me all the information. This man will be released by five today."

"Is that a promise, sir?"

"Yes, that is a promise."

"Thank you, sir," Shelly finally adds, as she breathes a sigh of relief.

"You are more than welcome. I suspect this will be the last we see of you. Am I right about that?"

"Yes, sir—"

John holds up his hand for Shelly to stop. "No, sir, I doubt very much this will be the last time we see you. I mean, unless you are replaced."

Shelly stares at him. *How can he say that to the ambassador?*

Once they are out of earshot of the embassy, Shelly asks, "How did you know to say that about protests all over the US and the world?"

"Do you really think I am just going to sit on the sidelines and ignore what is going on here?" Shelly remembers Carlos saying almost those exact words. "There are going to be protests whether they let

Alberto out or not. We have been getting information to the antiwar movement since before I even got here."

Shelly is surprised, but then realizes that someone has to be telling the solidarity groups what's going on here. Now it all makes sense.

"Thank you so much. The Gonzalez family will be eternally grate—"

"Not to mention all the teachers Alberto represents. Shelly, I met Alberto on several occasions. That's why I had to ask you to stay quiet. I know what a great organizer he is, and how much he is loved by his fellow teachers. If it weren't for his work, they would all still be living at home with their parents. They couldn't afford to rent, let alone own their own homes, if it weren't for Alberto Suarez Espinoza."

"Wow, John, I had no idea."

"Well, now you know."

"Do you mind if I leave now. I want to let Isabel and Abuela know, so they can meet him when he gets out of prison."

"Are you still here, Shelly?" John says, with a big belly laugh. "Take care, little sister. And remember this: I couldn't have done it without you."

She gives John a long hug and even kisses him on the cheek.

"Thank you, big brother. You will always be family to me." Then she runs over to a graffiti-covered wall and flags down a taxi. *Can't waste one minute waiting for the bus today.*

Chapter 38

Horrible sounds and smells

Shelly runs into the Gonzalez home. "Come on. We need to leave now so we can get Alberto a change of clothes."

Isabel releases a long breath. "Here are his clothes. Wait, did the taxi leave?" She runs out to wave the *taxista* to come back.

"Abuela, are you ready."

She puts her sweater on and walks over to the door. "Of course I'm ready." She gives Shelly a huge smile.

They run out and jump into the backseat. Isabel rides in front as she knows the *taxista*. *Small world*, Shelly thinks.

When they arrive at the front of the men's prison, Isabel pays the driver, giving him a large tip. *"Muchísimas gracias, Gerardo. Qué le vaya bien."*

"Dios les bendiga. Espero verles muy pronto."

Abuela stops for a second. "Isabel, shouldn't we have him wait? Alberto may not have the strength to take the bus."

Shelly is surprised by Abuela. *I wonder how many people she has visited here.*

"Si, madre. I will have Gerardo wait. I will see you both later."

"Shelly looks at Isabel, her mouth open, Don't you want to see your father?"

"Yes, I do want to see him, but not like this. Mother, you will invite him to the house very soon. We will have a big meal. We will have a celebration."

"*Si, si, hija*. Of course we will."

And Isabel is gone before Shelly can even see where she went.

Abuela and Shelly walk over to the guards. There is no line. This is not the time for visitors. Shelly says, "We are here to get my uncle, Alberto Suarez Espinoza. He is to be released today."

"*Perdón, señorita, pero no sé nada de eso.*"

"What? What are you talking about? Call the US embassy if you haven't heard about this release." The two guards look at each other and laugh.

"Chele, let me handle this ... *Señores, aqui tenemos el cambio de ropa.* We were told that you, kind sirs, would let us in to help him change and then he would be released."

"*Si, si, señora*. Yes, the paperwork is right here. Everything is signed."

Shelly stares at them, incredulously.

They walk over to the dark stairway, on the opposite end of the women's prison. As Shelly touches the cement wall along the stairwell, she notices it is black and smooth. *It wasn't like this at the women's prison.* Then she remembers the men with stained black hands and realizes that many more men have been up and down these stairways, many more than at the women's prison.

There are the same horrible sounds and smells as the other side, though, but with one added smell. *Oh my God, is that the smell of blood*? Shelly is feeling queasy. She fears she might faint.

"*Señoras,* we will give you an extra five minutes since he needs to get dressed. When we return in twenty minutes, the prisoner will have to walk out on his own. Do you understand?"

"*Si, entiendo,*" answers Abuela. But Shelly is horrified. She knows how weak Mayra was. *She would never be able to walk out on her own.* "*Está bien, Chele. Todo va ha estar bien.*" And Shelly prays that she is right.

Chapter 39

No more secrets

In the darkened corner of the cell, they see a slender man. They can't see his face.

"Alberto, is that you?"

"Si, soy yo," he says slowly.

"Alberto, it is me, Maria Elizabeth. Do you remember me?"

"That beautiful voice could not belong to anyone but my darling sweet Maria Elizabeth. Of course I remember you."

Shelly steps away from them. She feels like an intruder, but they don't seem to notice.

"Alberto, you speak like a man in love. Could it be that you have loved me all these years?"

"Of course I have. You are my one and only. Remember?"

"Si, por supuesto. I remember every word you ever spoke to me. I have gone over and over those words, looking for what I said wrong–"

"Ay, mi amor, you never said anything wrong. It was all about me. I promised your parents I would leave so you and my beautiful daughter could be safe."

"But Alberto, why didn't you tell me?"

"Because, my love, I knew if I ever saw you again, I wouldn't be able to leave. I kept my promise to your *padres*. And look how well you have both done."

"Alberto, that is not Isabel." She walks over to Shelly.

"Oh, silly, I know that! Your *norteamericana* friend is lovely, but she looks nothing like our precious Isabel."

"You have seen her?"

"Abuela, didn't Isabel tell you anything?"

"You know how my family is. I have to spy on them to find out anything about them."

"I am sorry, Elizabeth. Isabel and I decided it best if you didn't know we had met."

"¡*Ay, Dios mio!* The father of my child knows his daughter and everyone leaves me in the dark!"

"Don't worry about that any more, my love. From here on in, no more secrets. I promise."

And since Alberto has his own apartment and the union has kept paying his rent, they say goodbye with the promise to see each other again very soon.

Chapter 40

Shelly

Miguelito runs in the door of the victim's center with a shocked, almost terrified look on his face. *"¿Dónde está Ita Ceci?"* he manages to force out.

"She's in the courtyard," I tell him.

Then very quietly, almost whispering, he says, "Come, Ita Chele. *Ven conmigo.*"

"¿Y la camara?"

He shakes his head and I know it's bad. I know I don't want to see this, but I follow him anyway. We walk slowly; he's not pulling me this time. He's not pushing me. He almost seems reluctant. I grab his hand, hoping I can be of some comfort.

As we walk along the side of the dusty road, three army vehicles pass, going in the other direction, away from the scene of the crime. There are about fifteen people in a circle. I see the body but still know nothing. Miguelito is shaking. It is a hot day, so whether this is from fear or grief, I do not know.

The next time there is an opening in the crowd, I am close enough to see the dead body is a white man. *Oh God, please, don't let it be anyone I know*. I realize I'm praying. This place has shown me how to pray. More exactly, Abuela showed me how; El Salvador has given me a reason to pray. I have also learned to keep my thoughts and feelings to myself like everyone else here. If the army sees you care about the person they have killed, they may kill you too.

Ceci runs past us, crying. She reaches the body

before we even realize she is there. She lets out a long scream, then falls to her knees sobbing. I have to get to them. I must be whatever comfort I can be to her. I must keep my own feelings to myself. She needs me now. What do you say to someone who has just lost their soul mate in the prime of their life?

"Oh, Ceci, I'm so sorry." I hold her sobbing, shaking body. *Lord, help me know what to do, what to say.* I have never been good at this. Even back home, when someone died who had already lived a good long life, I was at a loss for words.

"John has been trying to prepare me for the possibility of this happening. I used to tell him, 'Don't be silly. You're American. They wouldn't kill you. It would create too many problems for them. They could lose all the US aid.' But deep down, I always knew that no one is safe here. No one!"

Out of the corner of my eye, I notice someone grab the camera as inconspicuously as possible. "Someone said he captured his own death. The soldiers killing him is on film," I hear a woman whisper.

"Do you know where to take it?" I ask, not knowing what else to say, but also realizing that I need to know where to take the film of Mayra if I decide to take the photographs.

"*Si, si, ya sabemos donde llevarlo.*" I take a careful look at this person, in case I cannot find Carlos's guy.

"Oh my God, how will I live without him?" Ceci cries out.

Chapter 41

Tears

Dragging herself back to the Gonzalez home after working at the victim's center and then seeing yet another martyr, all Shelly can think about is going home. *How do these people go on? After seeing family members, friends, and neighbors tortured, mutilated, and killed, how do they get out of bed in the morning?*

Shelly bypasses the Gonzalez home and heads for the mountains. She thinks of all the losses she has had. Of course, there was the rape that sent her back home, but that was the start of this journey. Then she lost her grandmother, only to find out she wasn't really her grandmother. But she was old and had to go sometime. Besides, that is how she found out about Winnall Dalton, who is her grandfather and possibly the father of Roque Dalton, this country's poet. *Well, at least he is the poet of the Left. Someday, he will be recognized as the Salvadoran poet, the one who represents all Salvadorans, not just the elite.*

No, the real losses have been since she's been here. John's murder has Shelly wondering if anyone is safe here. *And the American nuns; how could that happen in any country, let alone this so-called bastion of Catholicism?*

Once at the guerrilla campsite, Shelly heads right for Carlos's tent. He listens quietly as she tells him how sad it was seeing Mayra's life sucked out of her. He holds her in his arms as she recounts the horror of seeing the nun's bodies being dug out from where they were buried. But when Shelly speaks of John's death, she feels Carlos's tears falling on her forehead, commingling with her own before they drop onto her shirt.

"John was here. He photographed me, though he didn't know what he would do with the photos as he hadn't been authorized to take them."

Carlos rocks Shelly and they stay quiet for some time. Then he looks into her eyes and she feels all her aches and sadness float away. She is calm. When he kisses her, Shelly feels her heart slow and she thinks of all the times she could have felt this way but chose not to.

Carlos gently undresses her, kissing every part of her body, even her eyelids. They say very little. He sighs, then she sighs, then they both take a deep breath and smile at each other. As Carlos enters Shelly, she feels a wave of calm pass through her body and the past is left behind. *I have never felt so wonderful in my life. The rape is erased from my mind, my body.* The rape has become part of someone else's distant past, some stranger's memory, not Shelly's. She lost her virginity, not from being violated by a stranger, but from choosing to be with this beautiful, loving man.

As Shelly's senses come back to earth, she notices the smell of fire and hears the crackling of burning wood and the guerrillas talking quietly.

Chapter 42

Christmas Eve in El Salvador

Shelly opens the door and is surprised to find Ceci there. "Ceci! Come in." Shelly gives her a big hug. Mr. and Mrs. Gonzalez had instructed Shelly to invite her, but Shelly had assumed she had plenty of family to be with on *Noche Buena*, the most important holiday of the year. Shelly realizes that she has never bothered to ask Ceci about her family, even though that was the first thing everyone asked her. *Perhaps John was the closest thing she had to family.*

After hugging Shelly back, Ceci hands her a box of *pan dulce*, which Shelly takes a peek at, then licks her lips at the thought of eating some of El Salvador's best homemade pastries. Abuela hugs Ceci, and says, "Welcome to our humble home," then takes the sweet bread from Shelly to put out on a plate.

"Um, those tamales smell great," Ceci says, as the rest of the family come to greet her.

"This is the one time Isabel and I cook together. That way, we only had to stay up half the night," Abuela says. "Shelly learned a bit about Salvadoran cooking last night. I think she has decided to stick to American cooking." She laughs, then winks at Shelly.

"*¡Dios mio!* What else do I smell?" Ceci asks as she makes her way into the family room. Mr. Gonzalez gets up and insists Ceci sit in his favorite chair.

"Well, since I knew Abuela would be up half the night, I stopped and bought a turkey. Shelly hasn't tasted Salvadoran *chompipe*," Isabel says as she brings the kitchen chairs into the family room.

"Oh my, Chele, you are in for a treat," Ceci says as she gives Shelly another hug.

How does she manage? I would be in the mental ward if I had just lost the love of my life.

"I did have it once when I was with Manuel." Shelly notices Letty's eyes light up. "But I am sure Señora Gonz ... er, Isabel's is going to be the best in town."

"Speaking of the devil!" Shelly looks around and sees a blank look on everyone's faces. "There's Manuel now." Shelly walks over and gives Manuel a big hug. "Hey, nobody told me you were coming."

"Yeah, Letty wanted it to be a surprise," Manuel says. He walks over to Letty, who has just run into her room and is now coming back out. Manuel kisses each cheek. "The way the French do it," he says.

"Don't tell me you've been there too!" Letty smiles and laughs.

"Nah, but I met a few French girls in New Orleans," he tells her. Letty frowns, so he adds, "And guys too." He smiles, then goes to greet Ceci and the rest of the Gonzalez family. "But wait, where is Juan Jr., the superhero I have heard so much about?"

Shelly shoots Manuel a look and shakes her head.

"He should be here soon," Letty says, nonchalantly. They all sit down to eat. Señor Gonzalez says a prayer and they are all smiling, especially Shelly, as they pass the food around the table.

Juan Jr. finally shows up when they are cleaning off

the table. "Hey, don't tell me I missed everything?"

"Juan, you are lucky that your mother and grandmother cook enough to feed an army." Shelly looks pleadingly at Manuel. *Please help. Geez, I am so good at sticking my foot in my mouth.*

"Hey, Juan. I have been waiting to meet you. Letty has told me so much about you," Manuel tells him.

"Yeah, that must have been a while ago. As you can see, I joined the army."

"How's that working out for you?"

"Well, not good, since I did it to help my sister, and she won't—"

"Come sit down and eat, Juan, while the food is still warm," Abuela blurts out. "Wait, Abuela. I ... I ... brought company."

"That's fine, Juan, but who? And where are they?"

"*Gracias*, Abuela, but ... well, I told two of the soldiers to come by for a meal. They are from the same little town. All the soldiers here are away from home. The officers were all asked to take a couple soldiers home—"

"Of course, but where are they?" she asks again. "Bring them in."

Juan Jr. runs outside and comes back a moment later with the two soldiers. They look like boys; they are so young and acting so shy.

Abuela runs to get the milk she mixes from the box. "Dried milk is better than no milk, right, young men?"

"*Si, si, está bien,*" they both say, one voice indistinguishable from the other. So Abuela sets the three glasses of milk on the table. She serves Juan and the soldiers the turkey and tamales.

"There are some potatoes here, and—"

"It's fine, Abuela. Don't worry about us. Sit down and talk to your company."

Abuela takes a chair from the table into the family room and sits down. Shelly notices her hands are shaking.

Soon, Manuel and Ceci leave and Letty goes into her room. Shelly, Señor Gonzalez and Isabel stay seated in the living room surrounded by empty chairs, as Abuela moves things around in the kitchen, cleaning up.

Juan tries to make small talk with his charges, asking how they celebrate *Noche Buena* in their town. They answer his questions quickly so they can get back to the business of eating. They eat like they haven't seen food in days.

Chapter 43

A huge mess

When Shelly finds Juan in his room sobbing, all she can think is, *It's about time.* She knew the tough guy image he'd been portraying to everyone had to be an act. Letty had talked to her in detail of Juan's life, his frustrations. And Carmen had told her the rest, the things that even Letty didn't know, things that none of the family would ever know.

She quietly closes Juan's door behind her, then asks, "What is wrong, Juan? What can I do to help?"

"There's nothing anyone can do. I've made this huge mess of my life and there's nothing I or anyone else can do," he tells her.

"But surely something can be done to fix it."

"Can I fix the fact that I don't know my own father?" Shelly is shocked to hear that Juan Jr. knows that Juan Sr. is not his father, but she lets him continue. "Can I fix the fact that the love of my life left me because I wasn't man enough to be a father? Can I fix the fact that we don't have enough money to put my sister through medical school? Now I'm stuck in this fucking army in a country that's fighting its own people. Armies are for fighting foreign invaders, not their own population."

"Juan, first of all, it's not your fault that you don't know who your biological father is. Besides, Señor

Gonzalez has always been like a father to you."

"*¿Chele, de qué estás hablando?* I only meant that I don't know my father because he doesn't talk to me, doesn't explain why he won't go to his father for help. I don't even know his history or my grandparents' history either. Are you saying he's not even my father?" *Oh boy, did I blow it. The way he was talking, I thought he knew.* "Tell me, Chele, *dime lo que vos sabés.*"

"Juan, I'm so sorry. I thought you knew. I can't tell you who your father is. I was sworn to secrecy. And I've already broken this promise by opening my mouth. Señor Gonzalez agreed to bring you up as his son. Your mother made him promise not to ever ask about your real ... er, your biological father. He agreed because he loves her and he loves you and has treated you like his own since the day you were born."

"Yes, Chele, you are right. I always thought he was my father. But why hasn't he helped me more? Why didn't he get help from his father?"

"That's not about you. He has his own issues with his father. And Juan, I know you love your sister, but it is not your responsibility to pay for her education. She doesn't even want you to do that."

"Yeah, I screwed that up too. She wouldn't even accept my first paycheck. She said that it's blood money!"

"Well, what do you think about that?" Shelly asks.

"She's right! I'm taking blood money! You might as well call me a murderer! Oh, Chele, if you knew the things they want us to do, the things I've already ordered my men to do. And the things I've done myself ... because everyone's hands must be dirty. That's the rule! I even heard them talking about killing Monsignor Romero. What would Abuela think if she knew?"

Juan now begins crying uncontrollably. Shelly sits down on the bed next to him.

"Why didn't I see what was happening before? How could I have been so stupid? Now, I am the enemy too. Yesterday, they took me to the detention center. They made me watch as they tortured a man. He was barely even a man. He was a medical student. All he wanted to do was to help people. They made me hold the electric prod that they had put up his anus. Oh, Chele, I deserve to burn in hell!"

Shelly hears Abuela tiptoeing away from the door and she finally figures out that Abuela eavesdrops on every conversation in this house. That's how she knows everyone else's secrets.

She knows now what her grandson has done. Shelly has no idea what to say to Juan. He's right. There's nothing that can be done to fix any of this. It is a huge mess. As Juan sobs, Shelly takes his hand. She wants to offer comfort, but she doesn't know what to do.

"I saw Carmen the other day. She has her life, her family. She has a husband. If only I could be sure she were happy, but something about the way she looked at me ... She looked so sad."

"I know. She did what her father wanted her to do, but her heart has always belonged to you." Shelly is careful not to say too much this time. She is sure it would drive Juan to suicide if he knew he had a son out there.

"So, you see, I have made shit out of everything in my life. If the guerrillas killed me, then at least Letty would get enough money to get through medical school."

"Don't talk like that, Juan. Please." She takes him in her arms and holds him, not knowing what to say and hoping this gesture is enough to calm him.

"I'd probably mess that up too and end up a quadriplegic. Or the army would decide there was some inconsistency and refuse to pay my family." She is grateful he has talked himself out of that. It occurs to her that she and Juan are not that different from each other. They have both run away from every problem they've encountered in life. She lets him cry on her shoulders the way Carlos did for her two nights ago.

"It's going to be okay. We'll figure out something," she lies.

"Oh, God, please help me!"

At least he has that. I don't even have God to help me, since I only passively believe in some kind of power greater than myself.

Juan's sobbing makes her breast tremble which makes her entire body tingle. She realizes now that Carlos has awakened her sexuality. There was nothing to fear. The earth did not open up and swallow her. *These are beautiful feelings. Though my body is aching for Carlos, Juan is here and he needs me.* She raises his face up to hers and kisses him on the lips. She can feel a tingling sensation and a yearning to have this young man inside her.

"Oh, Chele, would you do this for me? I have been with no one since Carmen."

Shelly puts her finger to his lips. "Shhh, it's all going to be okay," she whispers. Some part of her really believes it when she says it this time.

"You are sooo beautiful," he says as she slowly takes off her shirt, then her pants. Then she moves toward him again and pulls off his T-shirt and unzips his army-issue pants. She kisses him the way Carlos kissed her, all over his body, even his eyelids. Juan looks at her with an expression of pleasant surprise and she wonders what he's thinking. *I don't care if he thinks I've done this a thousand times.* But he looks at her with love and tenderness as he mounts her. He enters her with so much tenderness, all she can think is how much she's missed all these years. *What was I so afraid of? This feeling is like heaven on earth.*

They lie together for some time afterward—she petting Juan's hair and chest, he with his head on her stomach, sleeping like a baby.

Then Shelly notices the sound of humming. Abuela is happily cooking in the kitchen. Shelly smiles, knowing these walls are so thin she had to have heard. *She has to be happy that I have helped her grandson heal from some mortal wounds. Juan and Carlos have helped me to heal too.* In this moment, Shelly knows that the rest of her life is going to be all right.

Chapter 44

Generation after generation

"I have spent my life keeping secrets," Abuela tells Shelly and her grandson. "I refuse to do it anymore."

I am so thankful that Carmen and I were not in this house when she told me her and Juan's story. Knowing the truth right now would do him nothing but harm. Someday, Juan Jr. will need to know that he has a son, but now is not the time.

"But, Abuela, how did you know?" Shelly asks, feigning naivety

"Oh, we old folks have many ways to find out things. Besides, I've been doing this since I was a child, since 1932."

It occurs to me that Abuela is not much older than my mother, though her difficult life shows in her face much more than mother's.

"The secrets we keep, repeat themselves, generation after generation. And our secrets keep us sick."

Abuela has so much wisdom. What does it take to become wise like that? Will I be wise like she is someday? Then it occurs to Shelly the irony of what Abuela is saying. Her family's secrets have been repeated in at least four generations. Although they started with her parents, Abuela has continued the secrets.

"Your mother must tell you the truth about your father, but you should know that it is my fault. If I had told your mother the truth, this wouldn't have happened. But you should know that Juan Sr. has always considered you his son. He loves you unconditionally."

"Then why hasn't he helped me? Why didn't he get his father to help us?"

"He has his own demons to work out. He needs to come to terms with who his father is and even—or especially—who his mother is. He has punished his mother all these years because of what his father did."

"Do you know her, Abuela? Do you know my paternal grandmother?"

"Yes, this country is not that big. And she deserves to know who her grandchildren are. Every year, I have taken her pictures of the both of you. She is the one person who I have always told the truth to. She considers you her grandson too. She loves you just as much as I do."

"I want to meet her, Abuela ... soon."

This time, Shelly is controlling herself. She takes deep breaths. She has figured out that her crying stops these brave souls from expressing themselves. She finally gets it. It is hard enough for them to speak the truth, without hearing this woman-child crying on top of everything else. *This is what my mother was worried about too. All along, I blamed her for not wanting to know the truth, but she didn't want to upset us: her grandmother, the woman she knew as her mother and her children.*

Chapter 45

Terror

As Shelly passes by the homes in the Gonzalez neighborhood after a day at the refugee center, Don Armando says, "*Apúrate*, you shouldn't be out this late. It's almost dark." He always comes out to greet Shelly as she walks by, and it's true, she usually is back home before now. Shelly picks up her pace a bit.

As she gets closer to the house, she realizes something is not right. The door is ajar and there is a bottle of Tíc Táck liquor on the ground by the door. Shelly drops her backpack and walks into the Gonzalez living room. She immediately sees Letty's face, wide-eyed with terror. The same two soldiers that Juan brought into the Gonzalez home are tearing off his sister's clothes, pushing her, telling each other how good this virgin is going to feel. Letty looks at Shelly and shakes her head. She is telling Shelly not to come in. In the midst of this horrible crime, she is concerned about Shelly. Shelly can also see that she is stifling her screams. *Abuela must be in the other room. She's trying to protect her too!*

Shelly has to do something. She cannot let this beautiful young woman be damaged this way.

She eases her way back out of the house. For a split second, at a loss for what to do. Then she remembers the gun. She runs to the side of the house and pulls off the screen. She feels for the gun. She feels on the left hand side: *Oh my God, it's gone!* Then she pats the ground on the right side of the opening. *There it is!* She grabs it and holds it the way she's seen in movies. *I must be convincing. They must believe I will use it.*

Shelly bursts back into the living room, holding the gun with both hands. *"¡Váyanses ahorita o' les voy a matar!* Don't think I won't kill you, you *hijos de puta!"*

Shelly remembers in this moment everything that her father taught her about shooting. *Take a firm stance so you won't get knocked down. Hold the gun in your dominant hand and use your other hand to keep it steady. Make sure your eye is lined up so you have the right aim.* Shelly swore she would never aim a gun at another living thing, but she cannot let them do this to Letty. *I cannot let her go through what I went through.*

The soldiers look at each other and release their grip on Letty. Her blouse is in two pieces on the floor. Her skirt is torn. She has blood on her face. Some of her fingernails are on the floor. Both soldiers have scratched up faces and both are suddenly acting timid.

"Era un error. Pensemos que era otra," the taller one blurts out. "We thought this was where the guerrillas lived." Abuela has woken up and come out of her room. Letty runs to her. The soldiers are zipping up their pants. Shelly is shaking so much she can hardly think, but she finally shouts, "If you don't get out of here right now, you are dead!" She manages to keep her stance steady and switches the gun back and forth between her two hands. One of the soldiers moves quickly to grab something and before Shelly can think, she pulls the trigger. The bullet skins his arm and he yells. Then they both run out of the house, the slightly wounded one holding his arm like it's going to fall off. Shelly thinks they are gone, but then she sees the other one, the one who wasn't hurt, in the

doorway. She raises the gun to shoot again, but he grabs the bottle of cane vodka and runs off.

Letty and Shelly look at each other. They both know they have to leave. Shelly is sobbing, telling Abuela, "*Lo siento*. I'm so sorry."

"You have nothing to be sorry about, *mi amor*. You saved Letty's life."

Abuela goes to the kitchen and begins making bean and cheese sandwiches, while Letty and Shelly throw some clothes into Letty's backpack. Shelly runs outside and grabs the backpack she dropped outside the door. After she dumps out her notepad, some sea shells and other stuff she's collected, Abuela takes it. She grabs every bottled drink she can find in the house and wraps them in a towel. She carefully places them in the pack; then she puts in the sandwiches. She throws in the leftover tortillas from last night's dinner. Then she smiles at Shelly, "*¿Quién es mas fuerte?* Who is stronger?"

"Yo, Abuela, I am strong," Shelly tells her.

"*Si, mi amor, tú eres muy fuerte.*" She hugs Shelly so hard she can't breathe. They both have tears streaming down their faces, but they are smiling too. Shelly saved Letty. Now they need to make sure the soldiers don't come back for the two of them.

"Chele, come now! We must leave," Letty shouts. Shelly hugs Abuela and they head out toward the mountains.

Chapter 46

Choice

Going up the mountain this time is much more difficult than any other time. Letty doesn't know when she will be able to return home. And Shelly is emotionally exhausted from the entire scene with the soldiers. The fear of Letty losing her virginity the same way Shelly did is what frightened her most.

"Thank God for you. I can't believe you were able to do what you did, especially considering that you are a pacifist."

"You are going to have to stay until Miguelito comes for you. No matter the temptation, do not go home if you haven't been told it's okay. Do you understand?" Shelly questions her as if she knows better than Letty what consequences could befall her.

"But, what about you? You will be easier to identify than me."

"Yes, that is true, but I may have to leave here quickly. Maybe it is time for me to go home."

"*Si, entiendo*, Chele. You are right."

When they get to the camp, Ana and the others come to greet them. Miguelito has already run ahead and told them they were coming. *Abuela must have found him and sent him.*

"Where is Carlos? I need to see him. I need to know what I should do. I can't figure this out on my own."

Ana takes Letty aside and talks to her quietly. The youngest of the guerrillas are talking to Shelly and smiling. They have become accustomed to her. They tell her that they know some words in English, "Hi. How are jou?" They laugh. Then, the oldest one says he has a message from Carlos.

"I lub jou," he tells Shelly.

"*¿Pero, dónde está Carlos?* Why doesn't he tell me this himself? Is he fighting?"

"*Si, señorita, la lucha sigue en el cielo.*" What does he mean? *Carlos is fighting in a place called El Cielo, the sky? I never heard of this place.*

Letty runs over to Shelly. She hugs her and says, "Chele, I am so sorry. Carlos is gone. He was ambushed when he was out fighting the night before last."

Shelly crumples to the ground. "Noooooo! This can't ... I can't ... Letty, I can't do this anymore. This is t-too much!"

"I know, Chele, I know."

Shelly runs into the tent where they made love the last time she was here. She finds one of Carlos's shirts and covers her face with it. She screams into it so that no one can hear her. Carlos's scent is still here; the entire tent smells of him. *Oh Carlos, how could you do this? How could you make me fall in love with you?*

This is what war is about. It's about losing your future before it even begins. It's about losing your life before it's even started. Carlos has a family. They will never know what a great and humane man he was. They will never know how passionately he loved these people. If only he could have gone back so he could make

Americans understand what we are helping to create in this country.

As she stands there in the tent, tears streaming down her face, Comandante Ana walks in. *"¡No tengo el derecho!"* Shelly manages to get out.

"Of course you have the right. We all have the right to love, and to love profoundly, as many people as we can in this short life"

"But he has a wife and child. I *know* his wife and child."

"All the more reason that we should be happy he felt love in his heart before he died. All the more reason that you should feel good that you were able to know him so well before he died."

Shelly realizes that Ana is speaking English, perfect English.

"Where did you ... learn English?"

"I was one of the fortunate ones. My family sent me to the US to study when I was a teenager, probably hoping to shelter me from all this." She moves her palm out, showing that she means the war.

"So your family has money."

"Yes, and connections to the oligarchy. If I were to do research, I would probably find that I have relatives in the ARENA party, but I don't want to know."

"Have you been back long, been here long?"

"I came back to study at the university, a fact my parents will probably regret the rest of their lives."

"Were you here when the army attacked the university?" Shelly asks, remembering those blurry 16-millimeter images that made her decide to come here.

"I was here, but I studied at *la* UCA. Word travels

fast here, though, so I was able to round up some medical students to help the wounded. After that, I could not just pretend I didn't know what was going on. It was all so blatant by then."

"Do your parents know you're here?"

"I could come out and tell them and they would forget they ever heard it. They don't want to know. They don't want to see or hear the truth, that the army is fighting its own people, the poor especially, which is already about ninety percent of the people, but also anyone who tries to help the poor is a target."

"So you must totally understand Carlos, leaving behind his family to stand up for these people? You both had a choice and this is what you chose."

"That is right. I'm sure Carlos's wife knows exactly what to do. I'm sure he prepared her for this eventuality."

"Are there many like you ... and Carlos ... many who don't have to be here?"

"Oh, I'm sure there are, but we don't announce it. But we do have to be trained and the *frente* can't pay for that, so many of us in leadership positions probably come from money."

"I never thought about that."

"There is so much to be thought about before we can begin armed struggle. It takes years ... decades, even."

"I feel so foolish coming here, thinking I could make a difference, then falling in love like a silly schoolgirl ..."

"Who was it who said, 'Never think that one person cannot make a difference ...'?"

"Indeed, it's the only thing that ever has. ... I don't know who said it."

"We are all making a difference. And we may not see it in our lifetime, but if each of us does what we can, it's like a ripple effect—eventually it will create change. Eventually we will have justice, not just here in El Salvador, but throughout the world."

"I suppose you have to think that way."

"We all must believe it ... so I fight for the women who cannot. I fight for the ones who do not have enough hours in the day to earn sufficient money to feed their children, who have to put their children to work just to make enough for some rice and beans for their family. How can we expect them to become politically conscious? Yet they do."

"Carlos taught me this from an American perspective."

"They aren't all that different really. We both come from privilege, but once you see the naked truth, you would have to be heartless to turn away and do nothing."

"Americans don't know the truth. They don't see this reality. Not unless they go looking for it."

"That's where people like you come in, Shelly."

"But what can I do?"

"You will know what to do when the opportunity arises."

Shelly remembers Mayra, sitting in that cell, half-dead.

"Thank you, *Comandan—*"

"Ana, just Ana is fine." She hugs Shelly hard and holds her for some time.

I know she is hugging me for all those who died and all those who survived the death of a loved one. I am finally seeing, feeling what I sensed as I sat in those history classes, arguing with the professors.

Shelly walks out of the tent and over to Letty. "Letty, I have to go back. There's something I must do. Wait for my message."

"*Si, Chele, aqui le espero,*" she tells Shelly. "But, Chele, there is something I need to tell you before you leave. You cannot tell a soul, though." Shelly thinks for a minute. Can she promise that she will see Letty before she leaves the country? She doesn't know.

"Tell me, Letty, just in case."

"Miguelito is Juan Jr.'s son."

"Oh my God, Letty! Are you sure?"

Chapter 47

The next day

Once again, Shelly wakes at four a.m., just as she did a few short months ago. She follows the same routine she did that day: she puts on two shirts and a pair of shorts under her skirt. Abuela somehow knows that she will need a large lunch, enough to feed her for dinner too. Shelly doesn't tell her that the food is for someone else. She does tell Abuela not to fix her breakfast this time. Shelly doesn't want to get sick again, whether from the stench and filth or from the fear.

Since she left Mayra her jacket last time, she tries to think of something else she could present to her, something that would somehow give her some comfort. Shelly still has one unopened package of underwear, which she throws into her backpack.

She pulls back the mattress on the corner against the wall. She remembers the relief she felt when she told Letty it was back there. Letty was fine with it and had whispered to her, "You must keep many secrets and tell many lies when your people are at war with themselves." Shelly wonders if the same was true during the civil war in her country.

Although the camera is made to look like a watch, it's too big. If Shelly were to wear it, she is sure they would have her take it off and would examine it carefully. Although she finds it disgusting, she wraps some plastic around it and goes into the bathroom. It isn't that much bigger than a super tampon, but its shape is what is going to make it uncomfortable. She pushes it into her vagina and hopes that she can find a way to sit on that long bus ride that won't be too uncomfortable. She walks out of the bathroom and into the kitchen.

Abuela takes her backpack and begins arranging the food and drinks. Shelly sits down to have a little bite of something. Abuela has made a huge breakfast, despite Shelly asking her not to. She also has sweet bread. Shelly grabs some sweet bread and takes a big swig of *café con leche*. She wants to eat the wonderful breakfast, but instead tells Abuela, "I'm sorry, but I have had a stomachache since I went to bed last night. *Pero gracias.*" She gives Abuela a peck on the cheek and heads out to catch the bus.

I am calm. I have thought about everything that could happen to me and decided it is worth the risk.

Chapter 48

Back at the Prison

Shelly gets through the frisking without a problem. She is sore, just as she expected to be. *The people on the bus must have thought I was one of those lazy Americans who don't care about what people think, just the way I used to be. Sitting up straight was too painful, though. It was a relief to finally get to the prison.*

This time, Shelly tries not to notice the stench and the moaning, though she is sure they will be in her dreams tonight. *How can one really ignore such horrors?*

The guard slams the cell door shut, and then puts the key in the lock. Shelly flinches as she hears the click. Mayra is lying on the cement that was used as a table during her last visit. "*Lo siento.* No one told me ... you were coming this time. Even if they had ... I wouldn't have had the energy to rearrange my cell."

"*Mayra, ya tengo la cámara.*" Shelly is whispering. Shelly pulls her shorts and underwear down far enough to allow her to reach up and pull out the camera. One corner of plastic is all she can grab, then finally it plops out. She is careful to fold up the plastic so it doesn't get dirty. *I would hate to get a disease on top of everything else.*

"I need to have you sit where there is the most light. Even with that, I will have to leave instructions for the film to be pushed when it is developed." She sets the cement mold as close to the light source as she can get it. She realizes these will be beautiful images of a very ugly scene.

"Just sit as comfortably as you can, Mayra. I am going to do this *lo mas pronto que' sea posible*, but I need to use all the film. I need to be sure that some images are good enough to be used."

"*¿Como lo va a usar*, Chele? Do you already know?"

"No, not for sure," she whispers, "but I hope we can somehow get them to the TV stations so that the American people will be outraged and insist Reagan stop all aid to the Salvadoran government. I sure wish Carter were still president. He would be more likely to stop it."

"If you need me to do anything, Chele, just tell me."

"Even if it hurts, can you go back a little so the light is on your face? Good. Mayra, whatever happens—"

Suddenly, Shelly hears the guard opening the door. There's nothing else she can do but place the camera on her wrist and hope for the best. "*Cuídate, hermana. Nunca te olvidaré*. You are an inspiration ..." but Shelly is too choked up to finish her thought. *I will never forget my sister who will probably give her life for this cause.*

"Señor, can I give her something, *por favor?*"

"*Rápido, tengo mucho trabajo*. I don't have time for games."

Shelly grabs the package of underwear, as well as the sandwiches from Abuela. She places them on the table.

"I will never forget you, *hermana linda*," Mayra says to Shelly through a tear-stained face.

Again, Shelly has tears falling down her cheeks. She knows that this woman cannot last much longer. Even if she does get released, the damage has already been done. She would probably die within a few months.

Chapter 49

Juan Jr.

There is a lot of activity going on today. There is fighting going on in three parts of the countryside and the guerrillas have come into San Salvador to pass out leaflets and talk to people about what life will be like when they take over governing.

Now is my chance to go after those *hijos de puta* who tried to rape my sister. Thank God Chele was here to save her, but I let those two into my home. If I cannot trust them, who can I trust?

I pull up to the barracks and they both are there. One has his shoulder bandaged up and his arm in a sling. They both look at me, then at each other. They can see on my face that I know. "Come with me. I have a job for you two," I tell them.

"*Si, Comandante.* But we have something to do first," the tall one answers back. The short one remains silent.

"No, right now! *¡Ustedes dos van conmigo!*" It is difficult to speak to them using *ústed* when I have not a grain of respect for them, but I must cover my anger until I get them alone.

I drive them to a remote area, all the time talking about a secret mission they are going to do. They are so stupid that the bigger soldier says, trying to justify what they did to my sister. *"Comandante, nos equivócamos.* We thought it was the house where the guerrilla family lived. We—"

"Shut up, *cabrónes*! Even if it were someone else's sister, do you think it would be okay with me? If you do, you know nothing about who I am. Why bother to explain anything to you two? I know the indoctrination you went through. We are all scum to you now."

"No, *señor*, it's not true. We respect you and all the officers—"

"You are just digging yourself in deeper. I don't want to be associated with those *hijos de puta asésinos!*"

I stop the jeep and tell them to get out.

"Pero, señor, we did what we were told to do. They told us to go to your house. They said it was a test to see if you were really with us, with them. I swear, *señor.*"

This I did not expect, though I don't know why not. There is nothing these *cabrones*, the military and the junta government, will not do. They killed Monsignor Romero and many other priests. They killed the American nuns. Of course they would hurt my family to see who I would choose.

"Alright, you sons of bitches, I am going to give you ten seconds to get out of my sight. If I can see you after I reach the number ten, I will shoot you in the back. *Entienden?*"

"Si, señor, perfectamente. Está bien." I am trying to remember if that short shit has ever spoken a word. He's probably smarter than this other idiot.

So I let them go. It is not their fault after all. They

came from the countryside with no training in anything, most likely fleeing the army themselves. But just to be sure I shout, "If you return to San Salvador, *les voy a buscar*. I'm going to kill you!"

"*Gracias, señor.* We'll never come back to the capital. *Le prometimos.* All we want is to go back home to our family," this time the short one shouts back.

I cannot be sure, though, that they won't come back. I am going to have to find a way out of this country. Back in the jeep, I hear one of the prison guards on the radio, "We have the *gringa saliendo de la prisión* with some weird *aparato.*"

They have Chele! I must go find her.

Chapter 50

Shelly gets caught

It isn't very hard for the guards to notice that my so-called watch doesn't look quite right. They take it off me and begin examining it. They are looking at it and saying maybe it could be a secret weapon or a tape recorder. They still have me spread-eagled against the wall when a jeep pulls up. My heart is pounding now and I realize that I have been praying; I am giving this situation over to God to do as he sees best. If it is my turn to die, I only ask that somehow my death ease the suffering of these people. *Please, God, do with me what you will, but let these wonderful loving people finally have some peace.*

"What the hell do you people think you are doing? Do you know who this woman is?" Oh my God, it is Juan's voice. *Thank you, God.* "Don't you know that this woman is related to the President of the United States?" he lies.

"No, Comandante, but we were just trying to protect her. We found this ... thing on her wrist. Someone could be trying to kill her, sir."

What a bunch of hogwash. They were just talking about how nice it will be to have a *gringa* in their jail, how much fun they will have with me. But I don't say a word. I make sure not to look at Juan in case our eyes give us away.

"Okay. I will take care of it from here. *Dámelo*," Juan says, taking the watch ... er, camera from them.

As he gently grabs my arm, I again thank God for all this country has given me. The will to live, but also the strength to die when it is my time. Juan helps me get into the jeep, and pulls away. He tells me, "Wave goodbye to them so they do not suspect anything." So I do as he says.

"Chele, we are in big trouble. I need to leave the country before the army finds out that I cannot be trusted. I will be leaving tomorrow morning to cross the border into Guatemala. You need to leave too!"

"Wait, I have another plan. We will go to the embassy to get permission to marry, then—"

Juan pulls over to the side of the road and looks at me. Then he finally says, "Chele, I couldn't ask you to do that."

"I know. But you are not asking. I am asking you. Can you spend *el resto de la vida* with me?"

"Oh, of course I could live the rest of my life with you. I fell in love with you the day I first laid eyes on you at the airport, but I knew it was an impossibility, so I shut the idea out of my head. And then, when we made love the other night, I just knew that I could love you until the end of time."

"Okay, then it is decided. We will get married. So let's go to the justice of the peace or the priest, and then we can rush to the US embassy to get permission to go to the US. Maybe we can get Padre Buenpastor to marry us."

"Chele, I promise you will never regret this decision. I will do everything I can to make you happy."

"I know you will. All you've ever needed was a chance to start over." It's all I've ever needed too. "But we have to get this film to someone who can get the photos to the U.S. press *now*."

I have to explain a lot of things to Juan while we drive around, taking care of the marriage. Plus, we have to get my film smuggled out. Ceci helps me with that. She takes me to the photographer, a young Salvadoran man I met one time when I went to develop prints. He promises he will get it to the news sources in a few hours. They insist that I have to get out immediately. I cannot tell them about Juan, so I just tell them *we* are getting out as quickly as we can.

We get the embassy papers signed. I tell them I have been living with Juan Jr. for several months, which isn't exactly a lie. He did live in the house I've been staying in. Then we go to Padre Buenpastor to marry us. Juan has told me that he let the soldiers go, so I send Miguelito to tell Letty to come home now.

Padre Buenpastor is pleased to marry us. He doesn't ask too many questions, but I am sure he knows he is complicit in some bizarre scheme. He does everything quickly, but beforehand, he asks several times: *"¿Católica? Vos sos Católica, verdad?"* I know he wants to hear me say yes, that I am Catholic. Besides, it's only a half-lie. Despite my never going to church after age five, my father had acquiesced and allowed my mother to baptize me. I don't know who took the pictures, but I remember seeing them all the same.

When we arrive at the house with the news,

Abuela greets us. She showers me with hugs and kisses and even thanks me. "Oh, Abuela, you should thank your grandson. I learned so much about myself from watching him. Plus, now I am officially a part of this family."

"*Si, si,* Chele. You are one of us. You are Salvadoran, *corazón y alma.*" *Heart and soul,* it sounds so beautiful.

Mr. Gonzalez arrives, with Isabel right behind him. Miguel must have found them too. Then Letty walks in. I run over and hug her and tell her, "We are now sisters, sisters for life, Letty."

"Yes, of course we are. We will always be sisters."

"Letty, wait to hear what Chele and Juan have to say."

We are all there in the living room, half the family staring at me with anticipation, the other half complicit with the secret.

"You tell them." I look at my husband with pride and happiness.

"Chele and I are married. I am going with her to the United States. But for reasons we can't go into, we have to leave now." Juan grabs me, smiling and hugging me, and I can tell that as filled with joy as I am, he is even happier. I remember my grandmother saying, "Shelly, the man should always love the woman more. It's the only way a marriage can withstand all the problems that life deals a couple: children, bills, jobs, and family like me butting their nose in." I smile, realizing how similar Abuela and my grandmother are.

Suddenly, I hear thunder and the sound of huge raindrops on the tin tub in the patio. I run outside to see what it looks like out there, and it seems as if the sky has split in two and is dumping buckets of water down on us. I look to see Ceci with her jacket over her head, running toward me. "Ceci, how did you know?" I ask, as she hands me a small gift.

"Miguel, of course!" She hugs me and says, "*Felicitaciones*, Chele. I know you will be very happy."

"Thank you, Ceci." I am tearing up now, thinking about John and wondering if she will get another chance.

"Now, now, Chele. No crying today."

"We won't be able to get to the airport 'til this stops. Besides, planes won't be flying out anyway," Mr. Gonzalez tells us. "And today is *el treinta y uno*, New Year's Eve. The pilots are probably looking for an excuse to stay a while longer with their families."

The rain pouring down in the patio reminds me of when my brothers and sisters and I were little and Grandma (Dad's mom) let us go out and play in the rain. "You guys might think I'm crazy, but ..." I run into the patio and raise my head. I let the water fall into my mouth and all around me.

Juan removes his shirt and pants. He is the first to join me in the courtyard in the middle of the house, the Salvadoran equivalent of a backyard. He lifts me up and we laugh and kiss. Next, Letty comes in and we stand there hugging and trying to drink the rain. Isabel leaves and returns in her slip and grabs Mr. Gonzalez's hand. We make a circle and all begin yelling, "Ceci, Ceci." Finally she jumps in too. "I'm already soaked so what difference does it make?" The circle gets larger. We are laughing and going around in a circle.

We hear a knock at the door. Before Miguelito can get to the door to answer it, in walks Manuel. Manuel spent enough time in the humidity of New Orleans to appreciate this chance to cool off and join the family. He takes off his hospital shirt and comes into the rain in his *playera* (or what we jokingly call a "wifebeater" back in New York). Manuel immediately walks over to me and I can see the disappointment in Letty's eyes.

"*Felicidades*, Chelita."

"*Gracias*, Manuelito," I joke back. I have come to think of him as my little brother; we have been through so much.

"I thought you would marry my brother," he tells me, though he doesn't look unhappy.

"Victor proposed to me more than once, but honestly, I know he didn't love me, not that way. And I didn't think he was attracted to me." I don't dare tell him that I am pretty sure his brother is gay. "I think he wanted to protect me. He wanted to keep me from coming here."

"Well, I guess you can see why now," Manuel says, hugging me and laughing.

"You better take care of my little sister, Manuel." I look at Letty and hope she hears me.

"Oh, don't worry. I have plans for that girl!" He pulls Letty over to us and the three of us embrace, then we get back into the circle again.

Ceci looks at Miguelito, the boy who to her is a little man because of all he does to help. "Come on, Miguel. Join us."

"*Pues, si*, Miguelito," shouts Letty. She looks happier than I have ever seen her. Her nephew is now part of the family. Letty smiles and winks at me. I give her a look that reassures her that her secret is safe with me. It won't come out until we are gone. I too fear Juan might feel he should stay once he knows he has a son here, a son doing the work of a man.

"Abuela-a-a, Abuela-a-a."

"*Pues*, wherever my *familia* goes, so do I." She comes in fully clothed.

It suddenly occurs to me that I had days like this with my own family, but I never knew how important such moments were. I promise when I get home, I will show my family how much I love them. This family has taught me that love is all we have. Without it, there is nothing. With it, we can move mountains. Maybe even save a few lives. I say a quick prayer for Mayra in her jail cell. *Please, God, help her to be free again, for however long she has.*

Chapter 51

Embrace

Finally the rain stops. Of course, everyone wants to go with us to the airport, but that isn't possible. That Oldsmobile is a boat, as my dad used to say about his, but is still not big enough to hold us all.

Abuela is the first to say, "I better stay. I could catch my death of a cold and I need to be alive when Juan and Chele come back for a vacation here."

"Thank you for everything, Abuela. I learned so much from you."

"Okay, *niña*, no crying. No more crying."

"But, these are happy tears. You really are my *abuela* now."

"*Vaya pues, mi amor*. I know you will take good care of my grandson."

"I will do my best."

"I need to get back to the Refugee Center. I have to look for a new photographer now!"

"You are like a sister to me." I start to say "big sister," but she may be younger than me so I don't know how she would feel about that.

"Okay, *hermana*. Go back and teach those *norteamericanos* what we are all about here!" I love the respect people have here for Americans, calling us North Americans instead of *gringos*. Even if we don't deserve their respect, which sadly, many don't.

"I'll do what I can. I promise you that. I promise all

of you that I will find a way to let my countrymen and women learn the truth." And I know I will too, though I have no idea what my work will look like.

Miguelito comes over and says, "*Adiós, Ita.*"

I grab him and hug him as hard as I can. Then I whisper in his ear, "*Nos vemos, muy pronto, Miguel.*" I can't help the tears, but no one can see them anyway, as I am soaked to the bone.

Miguelito looks at me, surprised. "*Si, yo sé. Y tu papá* will know *muy pronto.*" I have never seen a boy look so happy in my life. Letty sees it too, and I can tell that very soon the entire family is going to embrace this child and welcome him even further into their lives.

Chapter 52

Going home

On the drive to the airport, we tell Juan's parents as little as we can while making sure they understand that we are in a dangerous position and must get out of here as soon as possible.

The soldiers stop us a few hundred feet from the airport. I look at Juan Jr. and am grateful for the hat that he borrowed from a neighbor. At the time, I thought it strange. The soldier looks into the car. "What are you people doing here today?"

Mr. Gonzalez calmly explains that his son and his daughter-in-law are going to America for a honeymoon. He is smiling the biggest smile I have ever seen. "*Felicidades*," the soldier says. I can't believe it. I didn't expect to hear that come out of his mouth. He tells the other soldiers to let us go and waves the car on.

Juan tells his father to drop us at the entry to the airport. He grabs the bags while I tell them both good-bye. Then Juan Sr. gets out and gives Juan Jr. the biggest bear hug he can muster and tells him, "Son, I wish you the best this life has to offer. No matter what happens, though, you are always my son and you can come home any time."

"Yeah, sure, *Papá*. I know that. I know how much you love me. You showed me that in everything you did."

Well, my husband has grown up today. That's all I can say. Mr. Gonzalez pulls out a handkerchief and wipes my tears away. I think of my own father and how he used to do this when I was small.

Because of the rain, we are late for the plane. We run as fast as we can and are outside and up the steps before I can have a proper cry. It's okay. I will see them again. Hopefully, we can get back here soon and take Miguelito back to the US with us. That is, if he wants to go. It occurs to me that we may come back here to live, once the war is over. Who knows?

Once we're in our seats, the plane takes off. We are very lucky that they waited for us. The other passengers must live closer to the airport. Or maybe it rained harder in our little neighborhood.

I am feeling ill, like I am going to throw up. I unbuckle my seatbelt and once again run toward the restroom. On my way there, though, I see another young couple, this one a gringo and a Salvadoran woman. Bill stands up. "Shelly, it is so nice to see you. This is my wife, Magdalena."

I grab both her hands and say, *"¡Felicidades!* That's a great man you have there."

I look at Bill. "I am so sorry for the way I acted in the restaurant. It was very childish of me."

"No, I am sorry. You were right. These Salvadorans are very special people. And some of the things I was told may not be true."

I think of Ana and all the other Ana's that must be out there.

"And some of the things you said might be true."

"Yes, of course. There is always some truth, even in a lie."

"I have a new husband. We just got married too. When I have the chance, I will introduce you."

"That would be great. Congratulations to you both."

"Thanks, um ... I gotta go now."

Once safe inside the restroom, I bend over the tiny sink and open my mouth wide, but this time nothing comes out. I realize that my recent stomach issues were not just about the events I was witnessing, though I am sure they didn't help. I have gone to the airplane restroom three times now, not to urinate or defecate, but to vomit. I look down at my protruding belly. Then I look at it in the mirror. *I am pregnant!* I think about Carlos and I understand now why people keep secrets. It seems like the easy thing to do at the time. We don't realize how heavy that secret gets the longer time passes. Nor how we have to pile more secrets on top of the big secret, the lie that festers inside us.

I haven't told Juan yet. I know he'll be happy, but before the baby is born, I must tell him about Carlos, about the possibility that this baby is not his. Of course, I could wait and see what the baby looks like. If the baby has all Caucasian features, then I will know that Carlos is the father. That will bring into play many new issues, such as finding his family so they have a chance to know Carlos's child. If he has some of Juan's features, I could avoid the possibility of losing him by being silent. But silence is still keeping secrets; silence can be a form of lying. I have gone too far to go back now.

My mother kept secrets. I kept secrets. We all have our secrets, but as someone once told me: "secrets keep us sick." Abuela said, "the secrets we keep repeat themselves." Her family is a perfect example: she kept the secret of who Isabel's father was, and then Isabel had to do the same for her own son. It is a never-ending vicious circle.

Of course, it is not my place to tell other people's secrets. Perhaps Abuela and Isabel feel that telling their family the truth would hurt them more than help them. Isabel should tell Juan Jr. who his real father is, but it is not my place to divulge that to him. She will have to do that when she feels the time is right. But someday very soon, I will tell Juan that Miguelito is his son. He deserves to know this and his son deserves to be treated like family.

Juan Sr. is also keeping the secret of who *his* mother is. He is such a kind man, I don't understand how he can keep his mother from her grandchildren. But it is not my place to judge.

I will tell Juan about Carlos, no matter the consequences. And my child will know who his father is. I will try to tell the truth, no matter how difficult, for the rest of my life.

Stepping off the plane and entering the waiting area at JFK is a shock. First of all, it's culture shock to be back home after being away so long. It's not only my time in El Salvador. The time in New Orleans was so far away from this life too. I remember some of Lori's friends used to say, "New Orleans is a third world country." I used to laugh, though I could certainly see exactly what they were talking about. Being here now, it is crystal clear to me how unfair and unbalanced the world is.

The second shock comes when I look up at the TV. The ten o'clock news is showing my photos of Mayra. The newscasters are saying, "These photos of a young journalist imprisoned by the Salvadoran government are proof that it is time to reevaluate the millions of dollars in US aid being sent to prop up that government."

Then they show a video of Mayra in a wheelchair, being pushed by her family. She is smiling, but it is obvious that it is forced. She must be in a lot of pain. But she is alive! *Thank you, God. Thank you for everything: my life, my family, this amazing family that I am now part of. Thank you for making my sadness so great that I went to a place to be shown what sadness really looks like. And how we get by despite the overwhelming wish to quit. With love ... and the little things in life. The sound of a child laughing. The beauty in a mother's love, a grandmother's love. Even when that might not be your blood relative.* Love makes family, not bloodlines. The woman who cared for me when I was sick and gave me toast and tea, and made me lemon meringue pies. That woman may not be my real grandmother, but she is the only grandmother I ever knew. Abuela once told me, "Love conquers all." I laughed at her at the time, but she is right, Love does conquer all.

What will come out of this trip, no one can be sure, but I know that I've done something. I have made a difference, no matter how small. I am related to

Roque Dalton. I am related to all Salvadorans. We are all connected and each of us must find a way to help those less fortunate than ourselves. Roque and Carlos, and all those who lost their lives in the name of peace and justice live inside of me. *Qué viva El Salvador. Long live El Salvador. Long live the savior, the savior in all of us.*

Works Consulted

Dalton, Roque. *Antologia*. Madrid: Visor Libros, 2000.

Dalton, Roque. *Las historias prohibidas del Pulgarcito*. Mexico, D.F.: Siglo Veintiuno Editores, 1999.

Dalton, Roque. *Los testimonios*. San Salvador: UCA Editores, 1996.

Dalton, Roque. *Miguel Marmol*. Willimantic: Curbstone P, 1982.

Dalton, Roque. *Poemas Clandestinos/Clandestine Poems*. Willimantic: Curbstone P, 1986.

Dalton, Roque. *Small Hours of the Night*. Willimantic: Curbstone P, 1996.

Dalton, Roque. *Taberna y otros lugares*. San Salvador: UCA Editores, 2000.